TRUST

RHONDA M. LAWSON

Trust

By
Rhonda M. Lawson

Published by
Meet the World Image Solutions

www.mtwimagesolutions.com

Copyright © 2024
Meet the World Image Solutions

Cover design by Dr. Rhonda M. Lawson

ISBN: 979-8-9872429-1-9 (eBook)
ISBN: 979-8-9872429-2-6 (Paperback)

Meet the World Image Solutions

Dedication

To everyone who has ever had their heart broken and
had the courage to continue searching for love.
Protect your heart, spirit, and body.

ACKNOWLEDGMENTS

I finally did it! I dipped my big toe back into the literary world, and it feels great! Truth be told, I never really left the literary world. I just took a break to finish my doctorate, retire from the Army, move back to the United States, start my publicity and literary services company Meet the World Image Solutions, launch my talk show Horizons with Meet the World Image Solutions, and found the Black History Month Literary Weekend. Needless to say, I was a little busy!

As an author myself, I know very well what it means to need support in writing and promoting your books, so I started Meet the World to do just that. I am proud to say that we have provided editing and publicity support to hundreds of authors and entrepreneurs throughout the United States, Europe, and Asia. I've interviewed some of the most influential African American authors of our time. We have provided scholarships for middle school students and have donated countless books to schools and libraries. Starting this company hasn't been without its challenges, but I wouldn't trade in the satisfaction I and my team have received from helping other people realize their dreams. This is what it's all about.

Thank you to my dedicated team, Mrs. Louisiana Universal Clairica Newberry Lange, Ms. Amelie Rousseve, and, of course, my mother Phyllis M. Jones. You all recognized that I was doing too much by myself, and I will always appreciate the way you recognized and supported the vision, jumped in, and helped make Team MTW a reality! I especially appreciate my mother, who has always had my back. Thank you for believing in me, backing me, and even fighting for me. I don't say it enough, but I could not have accomplished any of this without your support. I love you! And to the extended members of Team MTW, Leslie Claiborne, Saran Bynum, Author/Chef Diana Riley, author and Black Authors Rock founder LaTracey Drux, my wonderful daughter and up-and-coming actress Beautiful Lawson, the entire Livious family (my sister, brother-in-law and nephews), and the countless clients who believed in me and trusted me with their exposure needs, I appreciate you and love you for all that you've done.

Yet, with all that we have accomplished, I couldn't help missing writing. Although I had edited and contributed to three anthologies over the last few years, it had been years since I'd written my own book. I missed writing stories that touched people and creating characters with whom my readers could relate and identify. I'd felt the pull for quite a while, but it wasn't until reconnecting with my sister of the pen Joylynn Ross that I finally decided to make my writing a priority. I will always thank her for that encouraging and motivational conversation. So, once the infamous COVID-19 quarantine began, I took the opportunity to dust off this old short story and get to work.

Trust started off as a short story for an anthology called *Crimes of Passion*. The anthology was the brainchild of fellow author Yolanda Johnson-Bryant, who pulled together an outstanding lineup of up-and-coming authors to create stories about crimes that happened in the heat of passion. I had only been in the writing game for about two years, so I was honored to be included, and was thrilled at the awesome feedback the book received. So, when Joylynn gave me the idea of resurrecting one of my old short stories as a way to return to writing, I knew *Trust* was the way to go. Major thanks to author John Wooden. I'm not sure this resurrection would have happened if it hadn't been for you still having this story in your files. I hope the rewrite makes you proud!

I would also like to send a shoutout to my *10 Pages A Day* Facebook family. I pulled this group of writers together not long after the quarantine began to help motivate them to pen their first books or refine the books they already had. However, once I began rewriting *Trust*, they wound up being just as much an encouragement to me as I thought I was being to them. I wish you all the best in your writing journeys.

Special thanks to my friend and forever sergeant major Nathaniel Flowers, and Dr. Henry Williams, my great friend and Greek brother, for reading *Trust* and giving me your honest feedback. It was important to me that men Beta read this novella so I could ensure that Saivon sounded realistic. I knew I would get the real from you guys and you delivered!

To the ladies who read for me, my Soror Nicole Butler of @butlersbookbag, Keyra Solei, president of Allure Book Club in New Orleans, my awesome sister and Soror Renee Livious, and fellow author and Soror Tracey Jackson, your input meant the world to me. Thank you for helping me to add more realism to the female characters. Everything you told me was crucial to the story.

So many people have shown me love and encouragement since I retired from the U.S. Army after 23 years. People like author Brian W. Smith, author Naleighna Kai, author Lisa Dumas Harris, my Soror LaRita Dalton, author and National Black Book Festival co-founder Gwen Richardson, author and publisher Toschia Moffett, fellow veteran Dr. Latoya Sizer, Soror Dr. Romanda Dillon, Soror Mary H. Carter, and way too many more to name. Thank you all for believing in me and never allowing me to abandon my first passion: the written word.

Last, but never least, I would like to send a special shout to my father, Nathan Jones. I love you Daddy, and you are in my prayers every day.

I know I missed some people, which is why I've never liked lists. If I didn't mention your name, please charge it to my head and not my heart. There are so many people I would like to name, but no one bought this book to read 20 pages of acknowledgements! It's time to end this and get into the story.

Not many people can say they've never met a Saivon. They've either been him, experienced being hurt by him, or helped pick up the pieces after someone they knew was hurt by him. He is an interesting character with a few layers, and surprisingly, some women told me they felt that he could be redeemed. You tell me: can a player be redeemed? Can the love of a good woman change him? Check out the story and let me know what you think on any of my social media handles: Twitter: @MTWImageSltns; IG: @meettheworldimagesolutions; Facebook: @MTWImageSolutions. You can also check out my website at www.mtwimagesolutions.com. We're still supporting authors and entrepreneurs!

1

"Oh, so now you wanna shoot me," Saivon said, staring into the eyes of the crazy woman standing before him. How could she even *think* about pulling a gun on him? This was what he got for messing with these weak ass women. The sex may have been easy to get, and it was damn sure good, but it wasn't worth the emotional bull that came along with it.

He continued staring her down. His best bet was to stay calm without showing fear. She was crying too hard to do any real damage. She looked scared. Too scared to pull a trigger. If he played this right, he could get close enough to work that gun out of her hand. Once he did that, he would knock the taste out of her mouth! His daddy always said if someone pulled a gun on you, they'd better be prepared to use it. He had no idea that he would ever have a chance to give someone the chance to prove it. Especially not a woman.

She held the gun shakily, trying her best not to show fear. She looked Saivon in the eyes, and he stared right back, his nose wrinkling in disgust. He folded his arms and shook his head. He really didn't have time for this. How long did she plan on standing there looking like a dumb ass?

"Nothing to say, huh?" he challenged, creeping toward his bedroom door. He shifted his eyes slightly. Why, oh damn why, was this happening right now?

She held her stance and aimed the gun directly at Saivon's head as she cocked the trigger. Tears streamed down her cheeks, but she refused to wipe them. Saivon had to admit he respected that. She showed heart, even though she'd obviously lost her mind.

"How could you do this to me?" she asked.

"Do what?" he spat, taking a step toward her. She straightened her aim, and he stopped in his tracks. "What the hell did I do to you that would cause you to act an ass?"

Her eyes widened. "Are you serious? You told me you loved me!"

He waved his hands in frustration and placed them on his hips. Was he being punked right now? "Are you fuckin' serious? You brought a gun in my house because you thought I loved you? Don't act like you never got played before. Get the fuck over it!"

"That's all you have to say?" she asked, taking a step closer to him, her gun still aimed at his head.

"That's all I'm *gonna* say. What? You want me to say I'm sorry? That it was me, not you? Grow the hell up!"

Saivon rubbed his head so hard he could feel the friction. This exchange was going nowhere fast. Maybe changing his tone would get that gun out of her hand and bring an end to the ordeal. He looked around the room, glad that his *real* woman wasn't around to see this. There was no way he would be able to sweet talk his way out of this situation. He had to get this bitch out of here, and he had to do it *now*!

"I loved you," she said, tears continuing to roll down her face. "I gave up everything for you. People thought I was crazy, but I stood by you. My friends wanted me to leave you alone, but I told them they didn't know you like I did. Why would you cheat on me? Why would you lie to me? You promised me there was nothing between you and her. Why would you propose if you didn't plan on marrying me?"

Saivon sighed and rubbed his eyes. He turned away and then turned back to her, softening his face. "I know what I said, sweetie, and

I meant all of it. But things don't always work out the way we plan. I'm sorry I hurt you. It really *is* me. I have some shit about me that I really need to deal with, and I shouldn'ta pulled you into it."

She held her aim, unmoved by his words. "This is so much deeper than that. Because of you, I lost friends. I lost family. I looked like a damn fool! I wanted to be with you so bad that I stopped speaking to everybody who had anything negative to say about us. I even considered getting pregnant so I could give you the daughter you said you always wanted. When you said you wanted to get married, I told everyone I knew about it. I even had the fuckin' China pattern picked out!"

Saivon forgot all about being gentle and broke into side-splitting laughter. Did he really have that much power? He knew his sex was good, but was it powerful enough to make women leave their families for him? He pictured her looking through catalogs for wedding dresses and wedding decorations and it made him laugh even harder. He looked around for the cameras. He just *had* to getting punked right now. "You did all that? I never even gave you a fuckin' ring! How you gonna blame me for you being stupid? Whatcha want me to do about it?"

"You evil bastard," she stated, her tears morphing into anger. "So now I'm the butt of a damned joke?"

He continued laughing, bent over as he tried to catch his breath. "This shit is hilarious. I'm sorry, baby, but killing me won't help you make better decisions."

"You never really loved me, did you?" she asked, her voice rising in anger. "You just used me to get your rocks off, right?"

Saivon let his laugh subside before he replied. "You fuckin' women kill me, you know that? All a man has to do is say I love you and you turn into a fuckin' doormat. Then when it doesn't work out, you wanna accuse a nigga of using you. Maybe *you* used *me*. You used me to get what you thought you were missing out on. All your other friends had a man, so you had to have one, too. You got tired of sleeping by yourself at night, so you used me to sex you down. And what about all those fuckin' bills I paid for you? Did I ever say no? All those times I told you I needed space, and you kept comin' back for more. You just had to have it. So, I say we broke even, wouldn't you think?"

Her arm began wavering, so she brought up her other arm to support the gun. Saivon winced, realizing he'd missed his chance to get that gun away from her. If he had jumped at her while she was trying to steady her tired arm, this would be a whole different story. He would just have to keep talking.

"Sit down and shut up," she snapped, darting the gun to a chair at the dining room table. He did as he was told, and then slumped in the chair and watched her, waiting for another chance to take control of the situation. If she was really going to shoot him, she'd have done it already.

"It's not about the sex or the money," she said, walking around him. She suddenly jabbed the nose of the gun into the back of his neck. "It's about trust. I trusted you with my heart and my life. When people told me you were no good, I refused to believe them because I trusted you. You used to tell me how much you loved me and respected me. You knew I had trust issues coming into this relationship, but you assured me that you would never hurt me. You told me I could *trust* you. You made me second guess myself when I knew I should have left your black ass alone!"

With that, she slammed the side of the gun into the back of his head. He leaned over and howled in pain, nearly falling out of the chair. She grabbed him before he went down and snatched him back up, slamming his back against the back of the chair. His head wobbled from the stars in front of his eyes. He eased his hand over the pain and flinched when he brought it back and saw blood.

"What went wrong?" she asked, walking back in front of him. "You were there for me when times were rough. You were a shoulder to lean on. When you told me to come visit you, I moved hell and high water to get there and be with you. You were my man and I wanted to be there to support you."

Saivon glared at her. Deep down, he really was sorry he'd hurt her, but there was no way he could tell her that now. He'd told too many lies. There was no way she would believe anything he told her. But even if he did want to apologize, she'd just butt-stroked him to the head. There was no way he would apologize to her now. *Crazy bitch!* If only he could just get to that gun before she got up the courage to actually use it.

"Look," he said, attempting to rub the pain from his head, "like I said before, things don't always work out the way we plan. It didn't work out. Just move on."

She rolled her eyes and straightened her arms. "It's not that easy. See, you hurt me. You lied to me over and over, even after I gave you the chance to be straight with me. You used me. You made a fool out of me. You care about nobody but yourself, and your ass needs to die tonight."

Now, he was pissed. "Bitch, if you don't give me that motherfuckin' gun, we're *both* gonna die tonight!"

With all the strength he had left, he jumped out of the chair and lunged forward, but she stepped out of the way just in time.

"What the fuck is wrong with you?" Saivon shouted, his momentum actually causing him to run past her. He turned around and ran at her again. "You want some dick or something? Would some makeup sex make your ass feel better?"

She answered him with a shot, hitting him in the arm. Two more shots rang out. Saivon's lifeless body fell to the ground, shock frozen on his face. As the blood puddle grew larger, a woman's scream filled the air.

2

One year ago

Saivon Lincoln. A handsome caramel-colored charmer with short, curly hair, the gift of gab, and a smile that melted the heart of every woman with whom he came into contact. Standing at only five feet, seven inches, his athletic build and immaculate dress made women forget about his height. He was soft spoken, leading many women to believe he was a shy guy. He liked it that way and played on it every chance he got.

In his opinion, his demeanor was what helped him win Carla's attention. He'd met her a few months ago when she began working with him in the administrative department of St. John's Hospital, a small privately owned hospital near Downtown Savannah, Georgia. Not shitting where you sleep was a rule that Saivon normally lived by, but Carla was so fine and quiet that he was willing to risk sleeping with a woman he worked with. He just had to figure out the best way to get close to her without scaring her off.

There was also the matter of getting close to Carla without half the department finding out. Most of the department consisted of nosy and messy women. One, in particular, was Angie, who was Saivon's current woman Anna's best friend. All she needed was a whiff of a *piece* of dirt and Anna would be on his ass before he could make it home. He didn't need the drama.

Opportunity finally rose on Labor Day at his friend Ronald's annual barbecue. Ronald didn't work at St. John's, but being a medical supply vendor, he was well connected. His side hustle was being a club promoter, which gave both him and Saivon unlimited access to some of the most beautiful party-going women in the city. The good part was that many of the women had a club mentality, so they expected one-night stands with no strings attached. That suited Saivon just fine.

Ronald's barbecues were legendary. He lived alone in a four-bedroom home in an exclusive neighborhood near Lake Mayer, so most women came wearing swimwear, even though no one swam. It was all to get an Instagram moment with trees and water, with the possibility of getting a professional man's phone number. The men knew this, so they always showed up wearing their best linen and Panama Jack hats, pretending to be unbothered by the half-naked beauty around them.

"You didn't tell me Carla was gonna be here," Saivon whispered to Ronald as they sat outside on lawn chairs, drinking beers. He bobbed his head as Frankie Beverly and Maze's *Happy Feelings* blared from the speakers and raised his bottle toward the DJ in appreciation.

Ronald smiled back. "I wanted to give you an early birthday present."

"Good looking out, dog," Saivon said with a smile, clinking bottles with his friend. His birthday wasn't until November, but who was he to split hairs? All he cared about was that Carla was there and Anna wasn't. He'd conveniently forgotten to tell Anna about the barbecue until the last minute. As luck would have it, she had to work so she wouldn't have made it anyway. And if she hadn't, he would have played dumb and made the excuse that he assumed her girl Angie would have told her. He chuckled at the thought because Angie wasn't at the barbecue either. Ronald hadn't invited her, presumably because he'd already invited Carla.

Saivon smiled as he watched Carla walk out of the house and stroll toward the drink area. She was cute, beautiful actually. He loved chocolate women, and Carla's smooth mocha skin definitely fit the description. The way her arms and legs shined from under her rainbow-colored sundress, he could tell that coconut oil was her best friend. And her hair! He loved a natural woman, and her twistout looked like a crown on her beautiful head. The fact that she wore very little makeup but still looked put together only completed the look. Saivon loved a high maintenance woman who made it look easy.

He studied her as she surveyed the beverages. Her drink choice would say a lot about her. She spent the most time at the alcohol station, so a whack ass soda was out of the question. If she chose wine, she might be bougie. If she picked up a beer, she may just be one of the guys, which wouldn't be fun at all. Liquor was tricky. It would depend on how she drank it. Was she a straight Hennessy girl or did she like mixed drinks? Was she an alcoholic or a social drinker?

He was impressed to see that she'd poured herself a small cup of wine. Just enough so she wouldn't have to make a return trip to the table, but not so much that she looked like a complete drunk. A little bougie, but he could deal with that. At least she had some class about her. That way, he wouldn't have to worry about her getting loud or running her mouth. She caught him checking her out, so he raised his eyebrows and mouthed, "Hey."

She smiled and waved back at him as she walked back into the house. Saivon nodded, kind of relieved that she didn't approach them. It may have made her look thirsty, which would have been a complete turnoff. He knew he would have her, but he at least wanted a little bit of a challenge.

Saivon had wanted to approach Carla for about a month, but she always had someone in her face. Many had tried to get next to her, including a couple of the doctors, but few had been successful. Saivon wanted to know why. He'd heard she had a boyfriend, but no one ever popped up at the office. She never received flowers. She ate lunch alone. He hadn't even caught her talking on the phone outside of work-related issues. He had the feeling she was single, but did anyone warm her bed at night?

"You better go talk to her," Ronald said, seemingly reading his friend's mind. "I think Bryon wants to get with her."

Saivon chuckled. "That nigga ain't got no game."

"You never know what a woman will fall for these days," Ronald replied before taking a sip from his beer. "Plus, you never know. She might be a hit-it-and-quit-it kinda chick."

Saivon took one last sip from his beer and then walked to the drink table. He returned with two Heinekens and gave one to Saivon before sitting down. The DJ had begun playing the *Cupid Shuffle*. People ran from all over the yard and lined up to perform the fifteen-year-old line dance as if it were just created yesterday. Carla was noticeably missing from the crowd. Both men opened their fresh beers, but Ronald set his on the ground, not ready to drink yet.

"Man, let me go check out this so-called competition," Saivon said, rising from his chair. Before walking away, he tapped the mouth of Ronald's bottle with the bottom of his, causing his friend's beer to bubble over like a fifth-grade model volcano. Ronald looked shocked, and then shook his head and laughed. Saivon chuckled as he walked off. He'd bring his boy another beer when he got back.

He walked into the house and headed straight for the kitchen. He glanced at Carla talking with Bryon on the couch. Instead of approaching her, he feigned retrieving ice as he surveyed the situation. Bryon had a stupid smile on his face, tracing Carla's hand with his index finger. She didn't look too impressed. Had she just shot Saivon a "help me" look?

Saivon had known Bryon, a doctor at St. John's, for years. Bryon also got his share of women, but he went about his dirt differently. He preferred the direct approach. Instead of taking a woman out for drinks or a movie, he preferred to just describe what he would do to her if he got her alone. To Bryon, all of the other bullshit was unnecessary. He'd once told Saivon that most women appreciated him being direct because half of them wanted the same thing. And the fact that he was a doctor only made it easier to get what he wanted.

Fortunately, Carla didn't seem to be falling for it. Saivon stifled a laugh and took the bowl of ice back outside and set it on the drink table. He then grabbed two more Heinekens and walked back to Ronald, who was lost in a chair dance to *Ain't Nothin' But A G Thang*. A bikini-clad thick woman with waist-length braids danced in front of him. Saivon recognized her as a nurse from a different hospital. She stopped dancing when she saw Saivon approach and gave Ronald a sexy wave before walking off.

"She seemed nice," Saivon mocked as he sat down and handed his friend one of the beers.

"She is," Ronald replied, watching her walk away. "Damn! God bless America."

The two men laughed and clinked bottles.

"That was quick," Ronald said as he popped the lid off his beer. "No luck?"

"Man, what's my name?" Saivon asked, smiling. "You know me. I don't get turned down. Bryon is shooting the shit out of his own foot. I didn't even have to do anything."

"Shooting that same tired game, huh?"

"Yep. I'll get at her soon."

A few minutes later, Carla came outside alone and poured herself another cup of wine.

"Kinda soon for a refill, huh?" Ronald called to her.

Carla looked around for the source of the voice, her eyes landing on Ronald and Saivon. She chuckled. "I just needed some fresh air."

"Yeah, I saw you in there," Saivon teased. "It looked a little hot and crowded on that couch."

Ronald looked down and shook his shoulders in silent laughter.

"And surprisingly you didn't catch my distress signal," she replied, placing her hand on her hip. She held up her wine with her other hand, making herself look like a model for Sutter Home.

"Sorry, I forgot my cape at home," Saivon replied, sending his friend into a fit as he rolled out of his lawn chair and dropped to his knees in laughter. *This dude knows he can be a clown,* Saivon thought as he laughed at his friend. "Hey, Miss Carla, lemme talk to you for a sec."

He rose from his chair and ushered Carla to a semi-secluded spot near the lake. "How you doin' tonight?"

"I'm good."

"You have a boyfriend?"

"Wow, you're direct," Carla remarked, visibly taken aback. "Is every man at this party on one tonight?"

"I can't speak for that nigga Bryon. I have no idea what you two were talking about." Saivon smiled shyly and softened his voice. *Time to go for the kill.* "I just wanted to let you know I like you and I was hoping to take you out sometime."

He thought he saw a look of relief wash over her face. Yep, he was in there. Sometimes all a woman needed was for a man to step to her correctly. Once he did, it was usually downhill from there. Now all he needed was for her to give the right answer.

"I'm sorry, but I have a boyfriend."

That was *not* the right answer.

"That's too bad," he said. He was disappointed, but he wasn't about to show it. He rubbed his head and smiled. "Well, if anything ever goes wrong—and I mean anything—you let me know."

She smiled. "I'll do that."

He was sure she would. As he backed away, he said, "Be sure you do. I'll let you finish enjoying yourself."

They went their separate ways, but this time Carla remained outside. Saivon again sat next to Ronald and watched as Carla stole occasional glances at him while talking with a group of administrators from the hospital.

"No luck, bro?"

"Just planted the seed, baby boy, just planted the seed."

3

Saivon knew it would only be matter of time before Carla came around. She claimed she had a boyfriend, but it was obvious that she was feeling him at the party. All he had to do was play it cool. There was no need to rush because he still had Anna.

He and Anna had been seeing each other for about three months. She wasn't the most beautiful thing in the world, but she was nothing to be ashamed of. Anna took care of herself. She worked out three times a week, and she didn't mind flaunting it. Her tan-colored skin was flawless, but Saivon felt she wore too much makeup. He also didn't like her "Weavie Wonder" habit, but he had to admit that her hair was always tight when they went out. It was like he was dating an Instagram model.

To Anna's credit, she had a strong mind. She rarely let anything get past her, which could be a blessing and a curse. Lying to her was a bit of a challenge sometimes, but thanks to his gift of gab and silver tongue, he knew how to pierce that wall whenever he wanted. And anything else he wanted to pierce.

"You hungry, boo?" Saivon asked Anna as they lay in bed watching Netflix. It was Thursday night, and he didn't feel like cooking, nor did he want a pizza. Anna, who's eight-year-old daughter was at her grandmother's house for the week, had been at his apartment for the past two days. Truthfully, her home was much bigger and nicer than Saivon's apartment, but he credited his silver tongue for making her want to leave her splendor to bum around in what he felt was a matchbox by comparison.

"Yeah," Anna said, rubbing Saivon's bare chest.

"Let's go get some food," he replied, rising from the bed and stretching.

"You don't have any leftovers in the freezer from that barbecue you didn't invite me to?" she challenged.

Saivon tried to hide his eye roll. He wondered how long it would take for her to bring that up. "First of all, why would I save food that long? That barbecue was three days ago. Anything I did bring home is long gone. Second, your ass had to work, so why you even trippin'?"

"You still could have said something," she said, turning onto her side and propping her head in her hand. "I didn't even know you were there until I saw the pictures on Facebook."

"Well, I didn't say anything because you had to work," he maintained as he peeked out of the window. It was a habit he couldn't help. Growing up in Chatham County always kept him on guard. "Besides, I figured Angie would tell you."

"Angie is not my man," she stated. "You are."

Instead of responding, Saivon turned from the window and walked back to the bed. He smirked and pushed her back.

"What? I thought you wanted to go eat?" she asked.

"I want my dessert now," he mumbled as he crawled onto the bed. He pulled the covers over his head and began sucking her secret place as he listened to her moan. That should shut her up for a while. The silver tongue struck again. They might just have to order Uber Eats.

4

"Hey, Saivon," Carla greeted as she walked into the office Friday morning. "You're in early."

Saivon had been walking to his desk with a stack of folders. Had Carla not spoken, he wouldn't have even seen her. The past few weeks had been hectic in the hospital. Pollen season was picking up, which meant allergies were picking up. With more patients filtering into the hospital looking for meds and quick fixes, and snotty nosed kids spreading germs both in and out of school, nursing hours had increased, and resources were depleting faster than usual. Saivon's section had been inundated with requests for everything from food service supplies to housekeeping needs. He had to come in early just to ensure he could get out in time to get his weekend started.

"Hey, Carla," he replied, slowing, but continuing his stride. Carla picked up his cue and walked him to his desk.

He'd purposely avoided the conversation they'd had two weeks ago, but now wasn't the time to bring it up. He still wanted Carla, but she'd have to wait. Schedules and equipment orders were the priority, which reminded him that he needed to call Ronald later.

"Yeah, I have a lot to do, and you know how folks always wanna leave early on Fridays, so I got to get my stuff done early so I don't get stuck out," he explained as he sat and dropped the folders on his desk. He looked at the folders and shook his head as pictured how busy he would be for the next few hours. If he played his cards right, he might be able to get everything done before noon.

"I hear you," she agreed. "I have a mountain of paperwork to climb, myself."

He looked up and gave her a blank smile. "So, you feel me."

"Yep. Well, I don't wanna keep you from what you're doing," she said, backing away from his desk. "Give me a call sometime."

Saivon smiled again and lifted his eyebrows, momentarily forgetting about his mental task list. His smile dropped a little when he caught a glimpse of Angie walking past. Her eyes narrowed to slits when she saw Saivon and Carla talking, but he shook her off and smiled again at Carla. He'd deal with Angie's nosy ass later. "How can I call you if I don't have your number?"

Carla froze for a minute, nervously shifting her eyes.

"I mean, uh, call me at my desk."

He chuckled. "At your desk."

"Yeah, um, that way, uh, you won't have to stop what you're doing if you need a break from all that paperwork."

He smirked, knowing she'd messed up. Had he broken down her wall without even trying? "Yeah, okay. I'll do that."

"Man, what you doin'?" Ronald asked Saivon over the phone that afternoon. "I gave Carla to you on a platter last month and you're bullshittin'!"

"Patience, baby boy," Saivon whispered, looking around to see if anyone was listening. He knew no one could hear Ronald talking, but it always felt strange to be talking about Carla and Anna in such small quarters. Angie was only a few cubicles away, and Carla was even closer. He scooted closer to his desk and cupped his hand over the phone's mouthpiece, as if it would muffle what he was about to say next.

"I got this, baby boy," he whispered, taking one last look back to ensure no one stood at his cubicle entrance. "I don't want her thinkin' I'ma chase her ass. I already asked her if she had somebody, and she said yeah. I already know she ain't really got nobody, but if she wanna keep playin' those games, I ain't gonna play them with her. I planted the seed. It's time for her to do her part."

"So whatcha gonna do about Anna?"

"She's good. I'll cross that bridge when I get to it."

"Well, you better hurry up and cross that bitch," Ronald said. "Bryon was sniffin' around again. I saw them together a few nights ago at *Friday's*."

"That old bitch-ass nigga," Saivon said, sucking his teeth. "She already wants me. He ain't got a chance. Let him spend all his money on her. She gone give me that ass for free."

"I don't think Carla is like that. From what I've seen, she's a grown ass woman with her head on straight. Be careful. Neither her nor Anna are nothin' to play with."

"I know," Saivon said. His cell phone buzzed from the other end of his desk. He glanced at his watch to check the Caller ID and rolled his eyes. *Speak of the damn devil.* "Lemme go. That's Anna calling now."

"A'ight, bruh," Ronald said. "I'll put your order in first thing Monday, but don't forget about what I said. Catch you later."

"A'ight, man," Saivon replied as he hung up the phone. His cell was on the third ring before he tapped his watch to answer and then leaned over to pick up his cell. He could never understand how people could hold entire conversations while holding their wrists to their ears. The whole thing looked *George Jetson-ish* to him.

"Hey, boo," he greeted, propping the phone between his ear and shoulder. He picked up an ink pen and attempted to continue his last schedule. It was nearly noon and he'd finish all of the goals he had set for himself for the day. "You good?"

"I'm great," Anna responded. "Just taking a quick lunch break while these kids take their naps. Sometimes this caregiver life ain't no joke."

"I respect you," Saivon said with a laugh. "I could never spend all day with a bunch of kids."

She was quiet for a moment, and asked, "Do you?"

"Do I what?"

"Respect me."

Shit, he mouthed, tapping the end of his pen rapidly against the folders scattered across his desk. "Where did that come from?"

"Nowhere," she quipped. "Just asking."

He pursed his lips and side-eyed his phone. *You're a goddamned lie.* But he couldn't say that without it causing unnecessary confusion. "Baby, you know I respect the shit outta you. You're amazing." He could hear her smile through the phone. "But you already know that."

"I know. I just wanted to hear you say it."

High maintenance ass. "You are one silly ass woman, you know that?"

"And you love every bit of me."

Saivon again pursed his lips and raised his eyebrows. "So, what's your plans for tonight?"

"Actually, that's why I'm calling. I have to drive Evie to Atlanta tonight."

"Everything okay?"

"Yeah, I just need to go through some paperwork," she explained. "My mom is working on her will, and she wants to discuss some things in person."

"You need me to come with you?" Saivon asked, hoping she would say no. He felt himself lean forward in anticipation of her answer.

"No, you don't need to," Anna replied. "It's not that bad a drive, and I'll be so busy with Mama that I wouldn't have much time to spend with you anyway."

He pumped his fist in silent celebration, reminding himself of Tiger Woods when he made a hole in one. He wasn't even sure why he'd offered in the first place. Ain't nobody feel like driving five hours to Atlanta.

"You think you can do without me for a couple days?" she teased.

"I'll do my best." It was a good thing neither Anna nor Angie could see him because there was no way he could hide his smile. He'd finally have a weekend of peace and quiet. No pretend family time with Annie and Evie. No parties. And no Carla. *Yet.* This would be a weekend of game-planning with maybe a club chick if things went right.

5

"Stupid, stupid, stupid!" Carla reprimanded herself as she paced her bedroom. How could she slip yesterday and ask Saivon to call her? She wanted to die. She was so embarrassed that she remained in her cubicle for the rest of the day, slipping out of the building as soon the clock struck 4 pm.

Her words and her lame attempt to cover them up continued echoing in her mind. No matter how many times she tried to divert her thoughts, no matter how loudly she played the car radio on the way home, her mind refused to let her forget how she'd nearly made a fool of herself in front of Saivon.

As soon as she got home, she crawled into her bed in hopes of letting sleep clear her mind, but the next morning, the memory remained. She felt like a teenager who'd been embarrassed in front of the cool kids.

She continued pacing her room, finally stopping in front of her full-length mirror. As she stared at her reflection, she flexed her calves by standing on her tippy toes. "There's a reason you decided to be by yourself. You don't need a man in your life right now. You just broke up with Shawn three weeks ago. Concentrate on you right now."

She and Shawn had been together for nearly three years, but the relationship crashed and burned when she realized she'd lost herself. She found herself putting up with behavior she would never have tolerated before, agreeing to things she would normally have debated.

There was nothing wrong with being a submissive wife, but Carla had never felt that her opinion was valued in the relationship. It didn't start off that way. They were happy at first. And maybe that was why she slowly began being overly agreeable, trying to salvage the love she thought they had. She believed he loved her too, but it felt like his version of love and a happy relationship was him shining while diminishing her light. If she had an idea, he had one better. If she made a decision, he would tell her why it wouldn't work. If she accomplished anything at work, he wouldn't celebrate with her.

Pretty soon, Carla found herself unable to make a decision until Shawn blessed it. Her friends thought she was crazy, but his overbearing ways had happened so gradually that she didn't realize how deeply she had fallen until it was too late. Her friend Lorraine constantly tried to point out ways in which she'd changed, but Carla didn't see it. Instead, she made excuses for their relationship.

The final nail in the coffin came when he told her he was moving in. *Told* her. He'd never even asked her how she felt about the idea. He'd just popped up on her doorstep with an overnight bag and never left. Soon, his overnight bag grew into a suitcase. After nearly a week, he began making space in her closet.

"Babe, you've been spending a lot of time here," she told him. "Everything okay?"

"It's all good, sweetie," he said as he swatted her dresses to the right. "Just figured that since we've been spending so much time together that we might as well make it official."

Her eyes grew into saucers. "You want to get married?"

"Eventually, when we're ready," he said with a laugh. "Right now, I'm thinking we should live together for a year or two first. You know, make sure we can live together first."

"Excuse me? Are you serious?"

Shawn turned and smiled at her as if he'd given her the greatest gift a man could ever give a woman. But something clicked as he tried to pull her in for a hug. Finally, everything her friends had been telling her started to make sense. Why would he make a major decision like this without talking with her? Why would he think it made sense to live together before getting married? How did he know that she even *wanted* to live together? Instead of joy, she felt rage. This wasn't how she wanted to take their next step.

"You're not moving in here," she stated, pushing him away.

He looked at her as if she'd spoken Arabic. Carla stared back in defiance. Yes, she dared to disagree with a decision he had made, and she wouldn't back down.

"You all right?" he asked, squinting at her.

"I'm fine," she replied, her voice gaining strength. "Are *you* all right? What makes you think you can make a decision to move into *my* house without even asking me how I feel about it?"

He opened his mouth to reply but thought better of it. Instead, he shook his head, rolled his eyes, and shook his finger at her dismissively. "You never did know what's good for you. I'm not arguing with you right now."

"Well, I know this," she hissed, crossing her arms. "I'm tired."

"Tired of what?"

"I'm tired of you squatting here. I'm tired of getting dismissed by you. And I'm tired of making excuses for the way you disrespect me. I can't do it anymore. You've got to go home."

They continued to argue into the night, even playing the silent treatment as they sat on either side of the living room. It was after midnight when they decided that they would stay together, but he would definitely go back home.

That was two months ago. Carla wondered if she would have handled things differently had she known that her view of him packing his bags and leaving her apartment would be the last time they would see each other. Although they'd called themselves still together, their relationship was never the same. Text messages went unanswered by them both. Phone calls were kept short. Events and outings were canceled. Carla knew Shawn was trying to punish her for defying him, but she was over it. So, three weeks ago, she called him to officially tell him it was over. He didn't answer, of course, so she left him a long voicemail, not caring whether he listened or not. At least she was free.

It was then that she decided that she needed to rediscover happiness within herself before she could truly give herself to anyone else. Until then, she would let no man get too close. As far as everyone at work knew, she still had a boyfriend and she planned to keep it that way. She'd broken down and gone to dinner with that idiot Bryon, but that was as far as that went. He was way too aggressive, anyway. Why would she give him some sex just because he took her to a mediocre restaurant? His conversation wasn't even that interesting, the food wasn't that great, and his sexual references were tired.

But this Saivon guy was different. What was it about him, anyway? He didn't push too hard, and they barely spoke, but when they did talk, she felt something. Nothing sexual. She just felt excited. He seemed confident, yet shy. Strong, yet humble. She figured that it probably took a lot for him to approach her at Ronald's barbecue.

She wondered whether she should try to get to know him better. He seemed nice, unlike Bryon, whom she knew was a player. Did he really think she didn't know he had been with three other women in the office? Believe it or not, *stupid,* women do talk to each other. No gossip had gotten to her about Saivon, though. Was that because there was none to be had, or was it because no one saw the need to tell her just yet?

Her cell phone rang, interrupting her thoughts. Lorraine's name shined from the screen as she picked up her phone from the bed.

"Hey girl," she greeted as she sat on the bed and kicked up her feet.

"Hey, girl, whatcha up to?" Lorraine replied.

"Not a doggone thing. Just sitting here thinking about how I 'bout made a fool of myself at work yesterday."

"What? How?"

"There's this guy who likes me at work, and I'm kinda attracted to him, too."

"Well, besides dating men you work with being a big fat *no no*, what's the problem?"

Carla laughed. Lorraine had the greatest talent for making the obvious sound painfully simple. "Well, besides that, I told you I'm not trying to get involved with anybody right now."

"I hear you, but what if he's "The One" and you pass up on him trying to wait for God to send you somebody?"

"I never said I'm waiting on God, Lorraine," Carla snapped. "I just said I needed to find myself. You know I put up with a lot from Shawn. I'm just not trying to go there again."

"I hear you, ladybug. I just want you to have some fun. I honestly don't think you should go there with this guy because you work with him. That can lead to nothing, but drama."

"I know you're right, but he's so cute and shy and smart and fine as hell."

"Shit, maybe I should meet him."

"Lorraine!"

"What? I don't work at St. John's. Ain't no need in both of us being lonely."

They both laughed.

"Girl, you are so stupid," Carla said. She loved her friend, but she knew in the back of her mind that if she had given Lorraine the green light, she would have shown up at St. John's first thing Monday morning to get a glimpse of Saivon.

"Just saying," Lorraine retorted with a laugh. "Now what did you do to make a fool of yourself? Did you get caught staring at him or something?"

"Remember the barbecue we went to a few weeks ago?"

"Yeah, I'm still thinking about that beautiful house. I wish I had gotten that guy Ronald's phone number."

"Focus, Lorraine."

"Sorry. Continue."

"Well, Saivon—the guy at work who likes me—was there, and he asked me if I had a boyfriend and I told him yes."

"What?" Lorraine exclaimed. "This guy was at the party? Why didn't I see him?"

"He was outside most of the time," Carla said. "Anyway, he pulled me to the side and asked me if I was seeing anyone, and I told him I was."

"I think I remember seeing you talking to some guy by the lake," Lorraine reflected. "You seemed fine, so I didn't pay you any attention. But I still don't know why you were hanging onto that so-called relationship with Shawn. Y'all were as good as broken up by then."

"Yeah, but we were technically still together, and I wouldn't have felt right pretending I was single."

"I can understand that. I still don't understand how you made a fool of yourself."

"That's the thing. He respected that I had a man and kept it professional since then, but then yesterday at work we were talking, making small talk, and I slipped and told him to call me later."

"You gave him your number?

"No! I don't even know why I even said that. Nobody even knows Shawn and I broke up."

"I guess that wishful thinking got the best of you," Lorraine commented with a laugh.

"I guess," Carla agreed. "But when he pointed out that he didn't have my number, I started stuttering like that boxer on *Harlem Nights*. Girl, it was ridiculous!"

Lorraine screamed in laughter so loudly that Carla had to take the phone away from her ear to preserve her hearing.

"Thanks for making me feel better, Lorraine."

"Girl, I'm sorry, but that's hilarious," Lorraine said once she finally got over her laughter. "Honestly it wouldn't have been as funny without the *Harlem Nights* reference, so thanks for the laugh." She chuckled again. "But seriously, Carla, it's not that big a deal. You just have to get back to being professional. As long you don't get all weird when you see him again, that little situation will stay in the past."

Carla nodded, reflecting on her friend's advice. "I hope you're right. I really couldn't take another embarrassing situation."

Monday morning, Carla walked into the break room and found Saivon and Ronald having an animated conversation with another guy she didn't know. She loved watching guys interact. They had a comradery that felt so different from women. Most women ran in extremes, either completely ignoring each other or cackling like hens. The cackles normally only came when all, or at least some of, the women knew each other well. But with men, they could act like best friends five minutes after meeting. It was fascinating to Carla.

Ronald was the first to notice that they had feminine company. He looked up and smiled when he saw her. "Hey, Carla."

"Hey, Ron," she replied. "Why are you in here causing all this commotion? Shouldn't you be at work?"

He laughed. "I *am* at work. I'm just checking on my people to see if y'all need more supplies. You not gonna rat on me, are you?"

"I'm no narc," she replied, drawing a few chuckles from the guys.

"She's just being nosy like the rest of the women in this department," Saivon remarked with a sly grin.

"Excuse me?" Carla retorted. "I don't think so."

"Well since she's in here, why don't we get a woman's perspective?" suggested the man Carla didn't know.

"And who are you?" Carla asked with a smile, turning to face the man.

"Oh, I'm Larry," he introduced, reaching out his hand to shake.

When she obliged, he added, "I work in marketing, but I come over here sometimes just to slum."

"Man f—" Saivon started. "You 'bout to get me fired up in here."

The men laughed again, and then Ronald pointed at Larry.

"This fool here thinks it's okay to ask a woman how many men she's been with before him," he explained.

Carla drew her head back in surprise. Why did men always ask questions they knew they didn't want the answers to? "Why would you want to know that?"

"You never know these days," Larry replied. "There are too many diseases in the world."

"I hear you, but how do you know she'll tell the truth?" Carla asked.

"That's what I'm tryin' to tell this fool!" Saivon exclaimed. "A woman ain't never gonna tell her man how many men she's been with. No woman wants to be looked at as a whore."

"Hold on, now," Carla said, turning to Saivon. "Why she gotta be a whore? Men get around just as much or more than women do. Besides, even if I told a man that I had only been with two men, he would never believe me anyway, so why bother? On top of that, no matter what number we tell you, it would be too many. You want your women to be pure as the driven snow, but like Fred Sanford said, who's doing the driving?"

This sent the men into a fit of laughter, causing some of their co-workers to send annoyed glances into the break room. Angie walked into the room and walked straight to Saivon.

"Can y'all keep it down before Mr. Renfro comes in here?" she scolded. "Y'all are really doing the most right now."

"Calm down, sweetie," Ronald teased.

"Umm, Ron, my name is Angela," she snapped, turning to Ronald. "Save the pet names for your hoes."

"And on that note," Carla sang, pivoting a one-eighty toward the door.

"Wait, Carla," Saivon called after her, ignoring Angie's attitude. "So, you would never tell your boyfriend, fiancé, or husband how many people you've been with?"

"I don't have to because I don't have a boyfriend, fiancé or husband," Carla reported too quickly. She regretted the words as soon as she said them, but it was too late. All she could do was remove herself from the situation. "Well, lemme get to work."

She scampered away, mentally kicking herself all the way to her desk. She'd done it again!

Saivon approached her about an hour later and sat in the chair next to her desk. Carla turned from her computer screen and nodded at him. The moment of truth had arrived.

"So, you're single now," he stated with a smile.

She smiled back. She'd been caught and it was her own fault. "Yes, I'm single now."

"Why didn't you tell me?"

"Well, I wasn't going to make an announcement," she laughed.

He laughed with her. "You didn't have to do that, but you knew I've been having a crush on you for a good minute."

"How would I know that?"

"I told you that at the barbecue."

Carla smirked and propped her chin in her hand. "You asked me if I had a boyfriend, and you haven't said much to me since then."

"I was trying to respect your relationship," he replied, his eyes trailing up and down her body. His gaze made her feel warm. "You must like a man to grab you and take charge."

She cleared her throat and shifted in her seat. This wasn't the same shy guy she was used to seeing. Could he see the steam from her collar and feel the heat in her face? *Fight it, Carla. This isn't the time or the place.* "Saivon, we'd better get back to work. I'm not ready for all that."

"Ready for what?"

"For…well…never mind," she said, waving her hand. She bit her lip and returned her attention to her computer screen.

"You're not ready to get with anyone else right now?" Saivon asked, his shy persona returning.

"Not really," she admitted, still facing her computer, although she snuck a look at him from the corner of her eye.

"I hear you," he said, nodding. "I can respect that. I know you just broke up with your man, so I'll just offer you my friendship."

She smiled, relieved that he understood.

"I tell you what," Saivon said. He waited until she looked back up. "A bunch of us are going to Happy Hour this Friday night. You wanna come?"

She thought about it. She hadn't been to a Happy Hour in months. Shawn didn't like her going to clubs or bars, so she abruptly stopped. He felt that going to places like that was disrespectful to her man, and that women in relationships had no business being there. Her love for him and her desire for their relationship outweighed her thoughts that his reasoning was the most ridiculous thing she'd ever heard, so she respected his wishes. Now that Shawn was no longer in the picture, she was ready to live again. "That might be fun."

"It will be," he said with a smile. He looked around and leaned closer to her. "We can get to know each other without the pressure. We can always see where things go from there."

Something below her waist jumped when she felt the heat of his breath near her ear. She hoped he didn't see her toes curl, and she was glad her brown skin didn't reveal the redness that had washed into her cheeks. This was definitely not a grown woman reaction. She cleared her throat and replied, "Okay, cool. I'll think about it."

"Don't let me down now," Saivon said, pulling a pen from her penholder. He found a piece of scratch paper on her desk and scribbled his number. "Call me later. I really wanna see you. I'll let you get back to work. I got a million things to do, myself."

He rose from the chair and lingered for a second. Before moving out of sight, he winked at her, immediately making Carla blush again. He definitely wasn't as shy as she thought. She wasn't sure if that was a good thing or a bad thing.

Saivon smirked and pulled out his cell phone as he walked back to his desk. "Whatcha smilin' all slick about?" asked a woman's voice.

He looked up mid-dial and rolled his eyes when he saw Angie glaring at him. Instead of sitting at her desk minding the little business she had, she leaned against the entrance to her cubicle with her arms folded.

"Do you ever take a break from being nosy?' Saivon asked. "Damn, girl."

He heard a snicker come from the cubicle next to her but chose to ignore it.

"I just asked you a question," she said, backing into her cubicle. "You ain't gotta get all smart."

"And you ain't gotta be in my business," he grumbled, continuing on to his own cubicle. He continued dialing the number. Ronald answered just as Saivon sat at his desk.

"The clock's in motion, baby boy," he said with a smile.

"All right, now," Ronald replied. "I was startin' to worry about you."

"Never that. By the way, she's coming with us to Happy Hour on Friday."

"What? Everybody from work is gonna be there. That shit'll get back to Anna faster than *you* will."

"Relax, I got it under control," Saivon assured him. "What's my name?"

"Just make sure you know what you're doing," Ronald cautioned.

"Watch me work," Saivon said. After hanging up with his friend, he leaned back in his chair and reflected on his conversation with Carla. He had to hand it to himself. He handled that pretty well. Maybe he should start giving lessons. That fool Bryon wished he could have half the game Saivon did.

His thoughts were broken by the sound of footsteps stopping at the entrance of his cubicle. Did Carla come by to experience more of his charm? He turned to find Angie staring at him and his smile dropped instantly. "Woman, what do you want?"

"Don't think I didn't see you smiling in Carla's face earlier," she warned. "Let me find out you're trying to play my girl like a fool."

6

Carla had been going at it non-stop for the last three hours, so when lunchtime rolled around, she couldn't wait to tear herself away from her desk.

She grabbed her lunch bag and made a beeline for the break room, rushing past Saivon's cubicle without a word. She pulled a soup bowl from her bag and placed it in the microwave, and then sat and chewed on an apple while waiting for the ding. Stacy, a fellow receptionist, walked into the room next.

"Hey, Stacy," Carla greeted between crunches.

"Hi, Carla," she replied with a smile. She took a seat across from her and opened her own lunch bag. "I saw Saivon talking to you at your desk yesterday."

"Yeah," she replied, trying to downplay the conversation. The microwave dinged, prompting her to rise from her seat and retrieve her lunch. She'd never noticed it before, but now she could see what Saivon meant about the women in their office being nosy. Stacy didn't waste any time trying to get the tea. No shame at all.

"Yeah, he seems pretty cool," Carla said once she was again seated at the table.

"Well, he's definitely nice looking," Stacy said, arranging tomatoes on her sandwich. "But be careful. I heard he's messing around with one of Angie's friends."

"Really?"

"Now, that's what I heard, but I would definitely ask Angie to make sure."

Carla nodded as she stirred her soup, a little annoyed because she could tell that Stacy was obviously fishing. How did Stacy know that the conversation between Carla and Saivon wasn't completely professional? It wasn't, but *Stacy* didn't know that, and Carla wasn't about to confirm anything for her. "I hear you."

As if on cue, Angie walked into the break room with a covered plate. She rolled her eyes once she noticed Stacy and Carla sitting at the table, and then ignored them as she placed her plate into the microwave.

"Good afternoon, Ms. Angie," Stacy greeted with sarcastic friendliness. She cut her eyes at Angie and pursed her lips. Carla shifted in her seat and silently ate her soup. "You good?"

"I'm fine," Angie mumbled, folding her arms and staring at the microwave.

"Those fiscal year projections got you too?" Stacy pushed, pumping her eyebrows at Carla. "I tell you. Between allergy season and the end of the FY, my husband is lucky to even get dinner. I go home exhausted every night."

Carla laughed. Angie cut her eyes at her and then turned to face her.

"Look, Carla, I'm only telling you this because I think you're a nice person," she told her, glancing at the door. "Stay away from Saivon. He's been with one of my best friends for almost a year now. I keep telling her to leave him alone because he ain't no good, but she won't listen. You think you're the first woman in the hospital he's tried to holler at? He actually got a woman in this department pregnant a couple years before you came. She quit because she was embarrassed. I see his bullshit every day, but Anna thinks he's supposedly changed. Don't get pulled into his shit. You're not special."

Carla sucked in a deep breath of fresh air. The room all of a sudden felt hot from the spotlight being shined upon her. Her soup no longer tasted good, so she pushed it away.

"Damn, Angie," Stacy said. "How long you been waitin' to let that out?"

"Shut up, Stacy," Angie snapped. "She needed to know. You were here when all that mess went down."

"Yeah, but, damn," Stacy stuttered. "You didn't have to tell her like that."

"No, I'm glad you did," Carla cut in. "There's nothing going on between me and Saivon."

"I hope that's true," Angie said as the microwave dinged. She pulled her steaming meal from the microwave and headed for the door. "I'd hate for you to get hurt behind some little boy trying to be a player."

Saivon was watching the news when his cell phone rang. He was confused at first when he saw an unfamiliar number but answered any-way. "Who dis?"

"Good evening to you, Saivon. This is Carla."

He smiled, noting to himself to actually lock her number in this time. He would have done it last night when she called, but he was distracted when Anna came over. *In fact, let me do it now*, he thought, tapping the speaker button so he could save Carla's number before he forgot again. "What's up, love?"

"Just calling to say hello."

"That's good. It's nice to hear your voice."

"Yeah," she replied, her voice trailing off.

"What's wrong?"

"You know, a few people saw you at my cubicle yesterday," Carla said.

"Well, I wasn't sneaking," he said with a laugh. He knew it wouldn't take long for the rumors to start flying. If those people could only mind their own business the way they minded his...

"I know you weren't, but some people had a few things to say about you."

"Yeah? Who?" he asked, already knowing her answer.

"Stacy and Angie kind of cornered me at lunch today. Angie wasn't too enthused with you talking to me."

He knew it! Good thing he was quick on his feet. His lie flowed like the Nile River. "I can't stand those two hens. They're always in somebody's business. Stacy is mad because my boy, Ronald, won't get with her. She's married, but she won't leave Ron alone. He keeps telling her he doesn't want that kind of drama, especially since he does sixty percent of his business with St. John's, but her silly ass can't understand that. And Angie thinks she has to watch every move I make just because her friend, Anna, likes me. Everyday, she finds a different reason to walk past my desk. I'm thinking about turning her in for harassment. The woman runs her own daycare business, but yet she finds time to hang out at the hospital. She can't be making much money."

Actually, Anna was doing very well with her daycare, and made enough to hire a manager. She had time to disappear from work for a couple hours, but that was beside the point.

"Angie's friend Anna *likes* you? You're not *dating* her?"

"That woman has been after me for a while. She used to spend hours sittin' at my desk tryin' to make conversation with me," Saivon said, making up the story as he went along. He tried to use as much of the truth as possible since he was sure Carla had seen Anna around the office once or twice. "I used to leave her sittin' there. I told her my boss didn't like her hanging out at the office. She used to pop up almost on the daily before you got there. Either cackling at Angie's desk or trying to play goo goo eyes at mine. Then she got my number from Angie's directory and started blowing up my cell."

"Damn."

"That's what I'm saying. Now, she has everybody thinkin' we're messin' around, but I never touched that girl."

"I hear you."

"If you and I ever get together, please don't tell anybody in that office. There's enough drama in that place and I don't want Angie or anybody else trying to cause trouble with us. I really like you and I don't want to mess up my chance to get to know you."

Carla was quiet for a moment.

"You still there?" Saivon asked, worried that he'd run her off.

"I'm here," she replied with a sigh.

"You okay?"

"Yeah. I just don't like secrets and drama. I haven't even been at that hospital long enough to be in anybody's drama."

"All the more reason to keep things quiet. I don't want you to be in anybody's mess."

He actually meant that, but not enough to stop pursuing Carla. He honestly liked her, but there were still some things he liked about Anna, as well. Until he could make a choice between them, he juggled the idea of keeping them both. That was only if Stacy and Angie hadn't ruined things for him.

"We'll see," she suggested, sounding unmoved by Saivon's words. Quickly changing the subject, she asked, "So what do you have planned for the rest of the night?"

He wanted to ask if she was asking so she could come over, but it was too soon. "Not much. Probably just watch this TV for a little longer and then head to bed."

"Yeah, I don't have much going on tonight either. I'll probably just holler at my girl Lorraine for a few and then read a book until I fall asleep."

Picturing Carla in bed with a book completely turned Saivon on. He never liked uneducated women. He'd have to explore this new-found information at a later time. Right now, he needed to clear his head. "Well, you enjoy your book tonight."

"I will," she replied, the smile returning to her voice. "You enjoy your TV shows."

He laughed. "That just made me sound like I ain't shit. You readin', me watching TV."

She chuckled. "I didn't mean it like that."

"I know you didn't. Maybe I'll go find a book to read, too."

"You do that," she replied, laughing again. "Enjoy the rest of your night, Saivon."

"You, too, Carla."

Once he'd gotten her off the phone, Saivon immediately dialed Ronald's number as he walked into the bathroom.

"What's up, man?" Ronald asked after the third ring.

"Hey, baby boy," he said as he turned on the shower. "Change of plans for Friday."

"Hey, Miss Lady," Saivon greeted Carla Friday morning.

She had just walked through the front door of the hospital and smiled when she saw him standing near the elevator. They had talked on the phone nearly every day since he'd invited her to Happy Hour on Monday. Well, except for Thursday night, when they'd played phone tag for an hour. He'd texted her, but by then she was over it and had gone to bed.

Carla had to admit that Saivon was growing on her. She'd begun feeling more comfortable around him. He was funny, understanding, and seemed genuinely interested in what she had to say. All week, her day started with a "good morning" text from him and ended with a "sleep well" text. Their conversations lasted at least an hour and were always filled with what she felt was meaningful conversation. She was getting to know him better, and she liked what she saw.

There was just one problem. As much as she was beginning to like him, she couldn't shake the feeling that she couldn't trust him. She wasn't sure if it was the warnings she'd received from Stacy and Angie, or if it was because she'd spotted Anna twice that week leaving the hospital. He'd explained all of that, but his suggestion that they keep their relationship a secret still bothered her. And then there was last night. Although Saivon had texted her, she couldn't help wondering if the reason they didn't speak by phone was because he was with Anna.

Stay strong and think with your mind, and not your heart, she told herself when she saw Saivon waiting for her at the elevator.

"How are you doing this morning?" she asked once she approached him.

"Better, now that you're here," he said. "Seeing your smile is a beautiful way to start off a day."

Carla blushed. He certainly knew what to say to please a woman. The elevator sounded when the doors opened.

"Madam?" Saivon offered with a sweep of his hand.

"Thank you," she said, walking into the elevator first.

Saivon followed close behind and looked around to make sure no one else got on. The doors closed, leaving them alone. He pressed the button for the ninth floor and moved closer to Carla. Then, without warning, he kissed her gently on the lips.

Carla looked at him with bucked eyes. "What was that about?"

"I'm sorry, but I wasn't sure if I would ever get a chance to do that, so I had to seize the moment while I had the chance," Saivon explained, using his fingers to wipe away Carla's lipstick. "Did I get it all?"

"You missed a spot right here," she said, pointing to the top of his lip. The bell sounded as the doors opened to their floor. "I should make you walk out with it on. Stealing kisses in the elevator."

Saivon quickly wiped the evidence away and chuckled as he walked to his desk. Carla pretended to walk away in a huff but couldn't help admitting to herself that she enjoyed the softness of his lips. He was definitely breaking down her defenses, and she was pissed at herself for showing him that it was working.

Anna walked through the office with an air of royalty. Her nose was held high, and her fake back-length ponytail bounced with her every step.

"Aww, shit," Saivon mumbled when he saw her approaching his cubicle. He glanced at his watch. It was approaching noon, which explained her unannounced visit. Something told him not to sleep with her last night. Every time he did, she played the clingy role.

"Hey, Von," she said, flopping into the chair next to his desk.

"Hey," he said dryly, trying to think of a way out of this mess. He was sure Carla had seen her bouncing her ass through the building. "What are you doing here?"

She drew her head back in surprise. "I thought I would treat your ass to lunch. You don't need to act all rude."

He rolled his eyes and tried his best to keep his voice down. Suddenly he had an idea. He leaned toward her and in a loud whisper, he said, "How many times I gotta tell you to stop poppin' up on me at work? My boss has been on my ass all day and I told you last month when you showed up that he didn't want you hanging around here. You've been here three times this week."

"I'm not *hanging around* here," Anna shot back, matching his low tone. "It's lunchtime. I was going to take you to lunch. Why are you trippin'?"

"I'm not the one trippin'. *You* are," he snapped. "You coulda called me and I coulda met you somewhere to eat. Instead, you popped up over here. You act like you don't give a shit if I get in trouble. Come to think of it, why *do* you come over here instead of calling?"

She didn't answer. Instead, she looked at him with a confused look on her face. Saivon smiled inwardly, happy that his plan was working. If he started an argument, she would leave without him having to say anything. He'd have her out of there before she could figure out what happened.

"No answer, huh?" he continued, leaning back in satisfaction. He smirked, knowing he had stumped her. Anything she said next would just sound like an excuse. "I know what it is. You don't trust me. Yeah, now that I think about it, that's exactly what it is. I work around all these women, and you keep coming around here to make sure I ain't tryin' to get with one of 'em. That's real fucked up, Anna."

She scrunched her eyebrows and looked at him as if trying to decipher something. She then rose from the chair and glared at him. "You know what? I *don't* need this shit. You obviously have something on your mind that you need to deal with. Go handle that before you call me again."

With that, she stormed out of the office, leaving a trail of curious faces peaking from their cubicles. Saivon also watched her leave. When he was sure she was gone, he sat back and chuckled to himself. He'd killed two birds with one stone. Anna would definitely stay away that night and he'd also made sure that everyone within earshot heard their exchange without having to raise his voice. Now, everyone would know there was trouble in Paradise. At least the couple of people who knew there was even a so-called Paradise to begin with.

His plan had worked even better than he thought. Carla passed by his cube an hour later. He waited until she passed back before speaking.

"Hey, Carla, why you walkin' so fast?" he asked.

She turned toward him while holding an armload of workbooks. "Just trying to unload all of this."

"Why don't you come back and talk with me?"

She looked around, and then looked down at the workbooks. "I have a lot of research, but I can drop by for a few. Let me unload this stuff first."

"Okay," he agreed. He had no doubt that she would agree to come see him. His real estate in her mind was growing.

She returned about thirty minutes later empty-handed.

"You over your lunchtime drama?" she asked, taking a seat in the same chair Anna had vacated.

"Yeah, that shit's probably all over the office," he mumbled with a dry chuckle as he drummed a pencil against his desk.

"You're right," Carla replied with a laugh. "Stacy told me before Anna even left here. I saw her walk out. She's cute."

"If you say so," he said, shaking his head. "But I don't wanna talk about her; I wanna talk about you."

"What *about* me?"

"Like when are you gonna go out with me?"

"Tonight. Aren't we all going to Happy Hour today?"

Saivon slumped in his chair. "I don't feel like being around all those people anymore. After that little show at lunch, all they're gonna be talkin' to me about is Anna, and I really don't feel like hearing it."

Carla nodded and squinted at him. "You sure you two don't have something going?"

He looked her into the eyes. "Carla, I'm tellin' you I never touched that girl. It's just a case of someone not knowing how to take no for an answer."

"If you say so," she conceded, "but I just can't see a woman running after a man after all these months unless he's doing something to encourage it."

Saivon sucked his teeth. "Don't tell me these folks got you drinking the Kool Aid, too. I thought you were better than that."

"I'm just watching my own back," she replied. "I told you before that I don't want to be in anybody's mess."

Saivon looked her directly in the eyes. This wasn't going to be easy. "Carla. I told you. Look, I don't want to be discussing my business here. Let's talk later tonight."

"Okay," Carla shrugged. "You want me to call you later?"

"No," he whispered. This was the part of the conversation he *didn't* want everyone to hear. He planned to keep this thing with Carla under wraps for as long as possible. He took her hand. "I wanna spend some time with you. Can I do that?"

She bit the inside of her cheek and diverted her eyes. "What do you have in mind?"

"Let me come over and cook for you tonight."

A wave of nervousness washed over Carla's face. "You want to come to *my* place?"

"Yes," he replied with a smile. "You don't have to worry. You'll be safe with me."

"Yeah, but—"

"No buts," he interrupted. "It's time we had a face-to-face conversation without all this whispering."

She raised her eyebrows in agreement. "Can you even cook?"

"Better than Paula Dean."

"Yeah, right," she relented as she wrote down her address.

It's just dinner.

At least that's what Carla tried to tell herself as she stood in front of her bathroom mirror. She touched up her makeup and shaped her twistout, all the time wondering why she agreed to let Saivon come over.

She liked Saivon, but there was something about him. Something that didn't seem quite right. He was attractive, smart, and very nice, but something didn't add up. She just couldn't put her finger on it. He had never been anything but respectful toward her. She remembered how shy he seemed when he first approached her at the barbecue. His easy smile gave him a boyish quality that made her smile just thinking about him.

But what about Anna? Carla wasn't sure she believed there was nothing going on between Anna and Saivon. Why would a woman hang around so much, only to be rejected time after time? Nobody but Steve Urkel had that type of tenacity. However, she was tired of discussing it with him, and she definitely didn't want to talk to Angie about it. If what Saivon said was true, Angie would never confirm that her friend wasn't involved with him. She'd probably lie just to keep Carla away. Besides, talking to her would bring more drama, and Angie had made it clear that she wasn't Carla's biggest fan.

Carla would just have to depend on her instincts, and playthings by ear. She promised herself that she would see what Saivon was all about without getting too caught up. That way, if her suspicions were confirmed, she could always leave him alone before any emotions got in the way.

"Lord, please make it happen that way," she mumbled as the doorbell rang. She glanced at her bedroom clock. It was almost seven. Saivon had arrived on time. She checked her reflection one more time and instantly regretted her outfit, shaking her head at her jeans and lady-cut graphic t-shirt. "Am I *too* casual?"

The doorbell rang again so the time for changing clothes had come and gone. Carla would have to roll with what she had. She waved her hand at the mirror and scampered to the door, mumbling, "Hell, this is *my* house."

"Coming!" she called out as she approached the door. Checking the peephole on the door, she smiled when she saw Saivon wearing a backward baseball cap and Polo-style pullover shirt. *He's cute.* She opened the door and saw that he held two plastic grocery bags. "You need help with those?"

"Nope," replied as he walked into the apartment. He greeted her with a kiss on the cheek. "Just point me to the kitchen."

Carla led him to the kitchen and marveled as she watched him work. She used to enjoy watching Shawn cook as well, so it felt a little strange to see another man standing at her stove. Saivon easily fell into a routine, preheating the oven and seasoning pork chops. Once he seared the meat and put it into the oven, he pulled a bag of fresh broccoli from one of his shopping bags and began chopping it into smaller pieces.

"Look at you, being all Bobby Flay," Carla remarked with a smile.

"Oh, I don't play in the kitchen," he replied as he rinsed off the vegetables. "My momma taught me and my brothers how to cook when we were young. She said she didn't want us depending on a woman to cook for us because too many women were too busy trying to be cute instead of takin' care of their house."

Carla drew back her head in surprise. "My mother told me something similar. She taught me how to cook because she said I needed to bring something to a marriage besides my looks."

"That old school parenting," Saivon said with a laugh. Suddenly he stopped and looked seriously at Carla. "So, can you cook?"

"Very much so," she replied, matching his intense gaze.

They burst out laughing. Soon, the aroma of roasted pork filled the air, bringing flutters of hunger to Carla's stomach. She began setting the table. "What would you like to drink with this feast you're preparing?"

"What do you have?"

"How about a white wine since you're cooking pork?" she suggested as she walked to the refrigerator. She pulled out a bottle of pinot grigio. "I usually drink this while I'm reading, but I guess I could share it with you."

Saivon smiled as he pulled the pork chops from the oven. He sampled a small piece and nodded. "I don't know a whole lot about wine. Is it sweet?"

"Not overly sweet, but I think you'll like it."

"I'm open to tryin' it."

Just as they began preparing their plates, Saivon's phone rang. Carla's eyes dropped to his pocket, wondering if he would answer it. He seemed to catch her gaze and fished out his cell. He set down his plate and walked into the living room. "Hey, bruh, what's up?"

Some of the tension left Carla's shoulders, satisfied that Saivon was talking to a man. She continued preparing their plates as he finished his conversation. After setting the plates on the table, she poured them both some wine and then sat at the table, waiting for Saivon to finish. She could hear him laugh into the phone as he strolled back to the table.

"Aye, bruh, lemme hit you back later," he said, his eyes fixed upon Carla. "I'm about to sit down to dinner with a young lady friend of mine…Nigga, don't worry about who it is…Let's just say she's a good one."

Carla smiled, knowing that last line was strictly for her benefit. She could tell by the way he smiled at her and winked while he was saying it.

"Sorry about that," Saivon said as he took a seat across from her. "My boy Ronald always seems to call at the wrong time."

"You should have told him I said hi," she said, propping her chin in her hand.

His eyes shifted slightly. "Now why would I do that when I was tryin' to rush him off the phone and get back to you?"

Carla laughed. His answer was bull, but she let it slide. "You ready to eat?

After dinner, they lay on the sofa and watched BET reruns. Saivon caressed Carla's soft afro as she laughed at episodes he was sure she'd seen at least ten times. He couldn't blame her, though. Martin Lawrence was still funny after all these years.

"I'm not sure what you love more," he stated once the show cut to a commercial break.

"What do you mean," she asked, shifting and turning her attention toward him.

"I mean, you seem like you read all the time, but you know these TV shows like you wrote 'em yourself."

Carla smiled and raised her eyebrows, and he knew he had read her correctly.

"Yeah, I spent a lot of time indoors when I was a kid," she explained.

"I was never really the outdoors type, so books and TV shows became my entertainment. I used to even watch *All My Children* with my mom."

Saivon laughed. "Don't feel bad. I still watch *Young and the Restless* and call my mom once in a while so we can discuss it."

"Now that's hilarious!" Carla exclaimed as she broke into another laugh. "I guess we have a few things in common."

He hated to admit it, but this actually felt good. So good that he nearly felt guilty for why he really wanted to visit Carla. This was supposed to be the night he made his move, but he didn't expect to enjoy the conversation. And he damn sure didn't expect to have memories of watching TV with his mother.

He wasn't falling in love. It was too early for that. But he was sure he was falling into *like*. What did that mean for Anna? She was also a good woman, even though she sometimes worked his nerve. Would his plan for juggling them both work out?

Carla howled in laughter as Martin and Pam fought the furry creature during their failed island vacation. Saivon didn't know what was funnier—the scene or Carla's laughing. He pulled her feet onto his lap and gave her a foot massage. Normally it was his secret weapon when he was ready to smash, but tonight the massage just felt right. The time for sex would come later.

Carla's eyes rolled back into her head as she lay back and enjoyed getting pampered. "Uuuuumm, I could get used to this. A man who can cook *and* give a good massage? This is too much."

"You want me to stop?" he teased.

"Hell no."

He chuckled and then they fell silent. The television was the only light in the room, but neither of them paid any attention to the show. Saivon watched as Carla battled drowsiness. Soon, sleep won. Her peaceful face looked so innocent. He could no longer help it. His hands stopped massaging and slowly glided up her legs, stopping at her waist. After a brief squeeze, they slid further up and brushed against her breasts as he shifted his weight on top of her. She awoke and kissed him.

The short, simple kiss soon grew into a deeper, more ardent kiss. As their kisses grew more intense, she held him tighter. They looked like two teenagers experimenting with sex, both afraid to take it any further.

"You know I've been wanting you for a long time," he huffed between kisses. His lips moved to her neck as he cupped her breasts. "Why were you playing hard to get?"

"I wasn't," she mumbled.

"Yes, you were. But that's okay. I like a challenge. You want me?"

She inhaled deeply and exhaled in jagged breaths as his kisses moved to her nipples. "Yes."

She pushed him away and stared at him. "I'm not trying to be hurt."

He froze and stared back at her. "I'm not trying to hurt you."

"Come on," she said, rising from the couch. She led him to her bedroom and pulled him close again. "What do you want from me?"

"I want all of you," he replied, undressing her. He eased to his knees and kissed her stomach. She wrapped her hands around his neck as his kisses headed further south. She felt tense at first, but soon her inhibitions began slipping away. This time was different. He didn't want to conquer her. For now, he just wanted to experience her. She was beautiful. For tonight, he wanted to make her feel wanted.

"Damn, you feel good," Saivon said, rolling back onto the bed. They'd just finished round two and they were both spent.

Carla marveled at how generous a lover Saivon was. His only mission was her pleasure. Between touching her in all the right places and sucking her toes, he excited her. She even loved the way he talked noise as he worked his way inside of her. Had she finally had a new lover?

She had to admit that he scared her just as much as he excited her. She still couldn't shake the fact that she couldn't trust him, but he made it so impossible to tell him no. Yet, her body spoke a different language. As good as he felt, she couldn't come. Was her body feeling the vibes that she tried to ignore? She wished she could will her juices to flow, but it wouldn't happen. Hopefully, because Saivon went down on her so many times, he didn't notice her lack of response.

"You made it good," Carla huffed. Despite her lack of an orgasm, she felt good. Saivon was an amazing lover, and as soon as she could get her mind to follow her heart, the sex would be even better. "You said you want all of me, but what are you really looking for?"

Saivon faced her and looked deeply into her eyes. He traced the curves of her shoulder and arms with his fingertips. "You see how good you're feelin' right now?" She nodded. "I wanna make you feel like this for the rest of your life."

Carla nodded again. She wanted to believe him. She wanted to feel that she'd finally found *the one*. But she was realistic enough to know that one amazing night of sex—even one that didn't end with a decent orgasm—was not a foundation for a meaningful relationship.

"Saivon," she began, shifting to her side so she could face him. "You don't need to say that. I like you, but I'm not forcing you to make me a part of your happy ending."

"What do you mean?" he asked, rolling back onto his back and staring at the ceiling.

"I mean, if you're not looking for a woman, I don't want you to think that just because we had sex that I'm going to be all up under you. We can keep this right where it is if that's what you want."

He turned again to his side and faced her. He looked sad. "Is that what you want?"

"No," she replied honestly. "I like you. I just don't want to be used, and I don't want to imagine something that may not really be there."

Saivon lay silent. Fear overtook Carla as she wondered whether she'd just run him off. How does a woman lose a man while he's still lying in her bed? *Dammit!* She tried hard not to show her inner turmoil, so she lay there and watched him as whatever thoughts he had flowed through his mind.

"Carla," he said finally. "I'm not going to lay here and tell you I'm in love with you. It's too soon for that. But I do want to get to know you. I want to know how you think. I want to know what makes you feel good. I want to be in your life. Whether we're friends or we take it further, I want to be in your life. Can you let me do that?"

And just like that, Saivon had once again made her feel like a giddy teenager. Her name sounded like cotton candy when it rolled from his tongue. He'd said all the right things, and it made her feel special. She hadn't felt this way since her early days with Shawn. Was this man too good to be true? Was he as wonderful as he showed himself to be, or was he just a good talker? Had she found a man who was true to the game, or did he just talk a good game? Was she still wounded over her relationship with Shawn, or was she ready to explore potential with Saivon?

"Carla?" he asked softly. "You still with me?"

She looked away as a tear stung the corner of her eye. "Yes."

He scooted over and spooned her from behind, kissing her neck. A chill ran down her spine. How could she feel safe from his touch while her mind was still in turmoil?

"Will you let me get to know you?" he whispered into her ear.

"Yes," she whispered as she wiggled deeper into his grasp. As their skin touched, she realized there was no other place she'd rather be. Maybe her suspicions were wrong this time.

7

"Hello?"

"Hey, Anna Baby, it's me," Saivon said.

"Look, don't call me with no more shit, Saivon," Anna snapped. "You cursed me out in front of everybody at your office, then you had the nerve to send my call to voicemail and turn off your phone last night. I don't know what your problem is, but you will *not* treat me like some bitch in the streets."

"I'm sorry, baby," he pleaded. "Girl, I'm going through some things at work. I didn't mean to take them out on you."

"Well, you did. Do I disrespect you that way? Do I ever come at you sideways?"

"No," Saivon replied, sounding like a child being reprimanded by his mother.

Then, don't think you can do it to me."

"Anna, I said I was sorry. I just needed some time by myself to think about some things. I told you I'm going through it at work. My workload is on a level twenty, my supervisor has been on my ass, and your girl Angie is on one every time she sees me. I love you, but sometimes I need some peace. You just don't understand."

Anna remained quiet for a moment. Her daughter Evie walked into the room and held up a piece of paper with a crayon drawing.

"Mommy, look what I did!" she squealed.

"Good job, baby!" Anna exclaimed. "You did good. I'll put it on the refrigerator when I get off the phone."

"Okay, Mommy," the little girl agreed as she scampered back to her play area.

"Is that my baby?" Saivon asked.

Anna rolled her eyes, refusing to answer. "Look, Saivon, I can understand what you're going through, but how am I supposed to know that if you don't talk to me? I just wanted to take you to lunch, and you popped off on me like I'm one of your little groupies."

"You don't get it, do you, Anna?" Saivon pushed. "I already told you my boss doesn't like you coming around. I almost cussed his ass out yesterday behind that fight you and I had. I'ma have to walk the line for a good while. I feel like quittin' that damned job."

"Don't do that," Anna said, her voice softening. "Don't throw away everything you've been working for."

Why couldn't she be strong when it came to this man? He always said or did something that softened her heart and made her feel like a damned fool. What pissed her off most was that she had every reason to leave this relationship, but then he would say something to make her rethink her decision.

To think, when she first met him, she wanted nothing to do with him. She didn't even like pretty boys, and with that curly hair and silky voice, he was everything that she *didn't* want. She hated the way he winked at her when she visited her girl Angie at the hospital. She hated her swagger that made him seem like he was God's gift to women, even if he never said it. She even hated how everyone thought he was so fine. In fact, the only thing about him that gave her pleasure was the fact that Angie didn't seem too crazy about him either.

"I don't trust his ass as far as I can throw him," Angie had told her.

"Why do you say that?" Anna asked. "Not that I want him, but if you have some tea that will justify me not wanting him, let me know."

Angie waved her hand at her friend dismissively. "Let's just say he ain't no good."

That was all Anna needed to know. The truth was, Saivon was cute. Damn cute. But he wasn't the kind of guy she usually went for. Pretty boys struck her as the types of guys who always felt they looked better than their woman. They would take longer getting dressed than she did and would stop and check themselves out every time they saw a reflection. She could tell Saivon was just that type, and she wanted no parts of him.

It wasn't until she met Angie at one of the hospital administrators' famous Happy Hours that she was actually able to get to know Saivon for more than just his looks. The restaurant was buzzing that night. It was Veterans' Day weekend, so there were a lot of Army Soldiers from Hunter Army Airfield and Fort Stewart crowded into the restaurant to kick off their four-day weekend. Anna had been approached by a few of the Soldiers just minutes after walking into the restaurant. One guy had actually captured her attention, and she would have gotten to know him better if Saivon hadn't plopped his arrogant behind next to her at the bar.

"I know you didn't give that buster your phone number," he slurred into her ear.

She could smell the beer on his breath before he uttered his first word. Her eyes traveled up and down his face as she wondered how he'd found the nerve to approach her in such a disrespectful way. "Excuse me?"

"You're Angie's girl, right?" he asked. His glassy eyes seemed to look right through her, and it made her itch. She winced and scratched her back. "I've seen you around the office a couple of times."

"Yes, and you are?" She knew who he was, but she refused to give him the satisfaction of letting him know that.

"Saivon," he introduced, jabbing his hand toward her. She took it and shook it like a limp fish. "You should let me take you out sometime.

I'll bet you I'm much more fun than that GI Joe-ass dude you gave your number to."

That remark actually made her laugh. She decided to go ahead and give Saivon her number. She knew she wouldn't hear the end of it from Angie, but she'd deal with her later. In the meantime, why not see what he was all about? Maybe he would confirm why she was never attracted to him.

However, when she called him the next night, he showed her an entirely different persona. He wasn't arrogant, nor was he the narcissist she thought he was.

"I'm sorry I acted like that last night," he'd told her. "I don't usually drink that much. It had just been a hard week, and people kept buying me beers, and I took them. I guess I lost count."

"I could tell," Anna said with a dry chuckle. "I could smell you coming a mile away."

"Damn, was I that bad? I'm sorry. I'm surprised you let me call you."

"Well, I started not to, but I figured I'd give you a chance."

"I appreciate your pity."

Their laugh together broke the ice and became the catalyst to their relationship. That was almost four months ago, and she liked to think they'd grown stronger than ever. Some nights they spent hours on the phone talking about everything from family, to work, to future goals. They spent nights at each other's homes, although he said he preferred her coming to his place because he didn't want to confuse Evie. Anna wasn't crazy about that idea, but she agreed, leaving Evie at Angie's home at least two to three times per week at first. However, once they grew closer, Anna would bring Evie with her to Saivon's apartment, which saved her from Angie's judgmental glares and passive aggressive warnings. Anna, Evie and Saivon would eat dinner and play together until Evie fell asleep, and then Anna and Saivon would go to his bedroom for their own alone time.

Evie eventually grew closer to Saivon, even giving him a Father's

Day card since her own father had shipped out to Korea without so much as a goodbye. Saivon was the only father figure Evie knew, which was why Anna felt she needed to hold onto the relationship despite Saivon's recent shady behavior. Although she would never admit it to anyone, she loved seeing Evie and Saivon together. It gave her hope of having the family she thought she would have with her father before he shipped out.

They had fun together, from nights on the town to Netflix and Chill nights. Anna felt like she knew Saivon better than anyone. Everything was fine until a couple of months ago. That was when he gradually began pulling away. She couldn't point out exactly when it happened, but their visits started being less frequent. He would say he was tired, or worse, he would make it seem like he was doing her a favor by breaking their date.

"It's getting late," he'd say. "I don't want you bringing Evie out in that weather."

Later, he started getting harder to reach by phone. He would go hours without responding to her texts, or sometimes he wouldn't answer until the next day.

"I did call you back," he'd told her just last week. "You didn't see the missed call?"

"There wasn't a missed call notification because there wasn't a missed call!" she snapped. "Don't play me for a fool, Saivon."

"Ain't nobody playing you for a fool, Anna," he replied with irritation. "Look, I said I called. If you didn't see the missed call, maybe something is wrong with your phone."

That comment pissed her off, but she was tired of arguing about the same thing. Angie had been trying to tell Anna to leave Saivon alone for good, and there were times when she really wanted to. But then they would spend time together and he would show her glimmers of what attracted her to him in the first place.

The night after she returned from her visit to her mother's home in Atlanta was one of those nights. Anna had already been emotional because her mother spent the entire weekend giving her a hard time about letting Evie spend so much time with Saivon. Her mother hadn't even met Saivon, yet she was convinced that he had no business in their lives. She claimed that he hadn't shown her anything.

Anna returned to Savannah completely depressed, so she left Evie at Angie's house and went straight to Saivon's apartment. She just needed him to reassure her that she wasn't crazy for holding onto him. And he did just that. He hugged her, fixed her some ice cream, and gave her a foot massage while she ate it. They didn't even have sex that night. Instead, he held her while they slept on the couch. She felt completely safe.

Why he couldn't be that way all the time was beyond her. Here they were just five days after that wonderful night, and they were arguing about a missed phone call. Maybe Angie and her mother were right. Maybe this relationship wasn't worth saving after all.

Anna sighed as she decided to drop the bomb she'd been holding onto all week. "You know, Angie told me she heard you were trying to get with some girl named Carla that works with you."

"See?" Saivon shouted. "That's what the fuck I'm talkin' 'bout! Nosy ass motherfuckers! I say hi to that woman when I see her, now everybody thinks I'm fuckin' her."

"Who said anything about you fuckin' her? I just told you what Angie told me."

Saivon fell silent for a moment, and then stuttered, "T-that's what they all think. T-this ain't the first time they accused me of trying to get with somebody. The same thing happened a few months before I met you. People act like a man and woman can't be friends. It's like they don't want me to be happy. Like I'm not capable of having one woman."

Anna sucked her teeth, not knowing what to believe. She would just have to keep him close. The truth would reveal itself sooner or later. "I trust you, Von. Just don't keep putting yourself in those positions to get talked about. And don't lie to me. I told you when I first met you that lying to me would be the worst thing you could do to me."

Saivon refused to heed that advice. Since spending that Friday night with Carla, she'd become a mainstay. He'd forgotten what it was like to be with a woman who didn't have children. Carla had a spontaneity that Anna could never have. They ate lunch together at least twice a week, and every once in a while, he'd talk her into being adventurous and sneaking off to spend the night in neighboring Hilton Head. On days when time was tight, he'd have her do the teenager thing and they'd settle for a quickie in the backseat of his car. It was fun, and it had been a long time since he could say that.

Time would only tell if Carla would become Anna's replacement. Despite their recent problems, Anna still brought a lot to the table. She was smart, pretty, a great mother, and she was a successful entrepreneur. To many, she was the full package. But Saivon wasn't sure he was ready for that yet. He loved the thrill of being with different women. He couldn't imagine letting one beautiful woman pass just because he happened to be with another. No woman was capable of giving him everything he wanted, so until he could find someone who at least came close—which would most likely be never—he would continue playing the field.

He'd realized his love for the game when he was still in high school. That was when he was a good guy with one girlfriend. She never left him or cheated on him, but he always noticed the attention she gave the so-called players. The athletes. The ballers. The pretty boys. She would pretend to be irritated by their presence, but the very fact that she couldn't stop commenting on them told him all he needed to know. Those guys might have been the players, but they also commanded respect and attention. The rooms would light up when they walked in. The girls wanted to be with them, and the guys wanted to *be* them.

Saivon always had the smooth tan skin and curly hair going for him, do he was no slouch, but he didn't have the swagger the other guys had. Soon, he began studying their moves with the girls, noticing the way they sweet-talked them into doing their bidding, and noting how they glided when they walked the halls. Their confidence was mesmerizing.

Once Saivon left for college and he and his girlfriend went their separate ways, he decided to reinvent himself. Instead of looking for someone new, he would imitate the guys he saw in high school, but do it better. He already had the looks and athletic build. All he needed to do was put what he'd learned into practice.

The first few ladies were the toughest. Attracting them wasn't the problem. Catching feelings was the issue. He'd attracted some bad women with great bodies and beautiful faces. The closer they got to him, the more they confided in him, and at first, he found himself growing closer to them and calling them more than he should. He didn't want to fall in love. It was too early in the game, and he still had a lot to learn.

However, the night he got caught would be a gamechanger for him. It was his junior year, and he was chilling in his dorm with his side piece when his roommate's hating ass let his main girl in. Of course, both women popped off at each other, and some furniture got pushed around as they yelled at each other, but just short of them throwing blows, he took control of the situation.

"Tasha, what the hell do you think you're doing?" he shouted at his main girl while catching her fist mid-punch. He turned to his side piece, who had cowered behind him. *Punk ass.* "Zina, go home. I'll call you later."

"What the hell do you mean, you'll call that bitch later?" Tasha shouted. "What is she even doing here?"

"She's doing what you apparently didn't have time to do," Saivon retorted, surprising himself. It wasn't what he'd planned to say, but damn, it sounded good!

"Excuse me?" Tasha asked, momentarily forgetting about the other woman who had scurried by her. A door slam told them both that she was gone.

"You heard me," Saivon said, gaining confidence. He walked up on her, anger written all over his face. "You've been acting real brand new lately, always actin' like you don't have time for a brotha. How many times am I supposed to get rejected? Don't get mad when the next girl wants to give me the attention you didn't wanna give me."

At that point, the entire conversation changed. Tasha had forgotten all about crucifying Saivon for cheating on her. She was too busy defending herself for not being the woman he thought she should be. Before the night was over, Tasha was in his bed promising never to neglect him again. The next morning, Saivon apologized to Zina and had her back in his bed by the weekend. As for his roommate, a good cursing out did a whole lot of good. They're still friends to this day.

The chess game he played with women was intriguing. It always amazed him how much shit a woman was willing to overlook just for the sake of having a man. And when he offered to pay a couple of bills for them, it was all she wrote! These women thought they'd hit the jackpot and put up with even more shit, convincing themselves that they had a man with money. Often, he didn't even have to come up with a good lie. The woman would hear what she wanted to hear, even when the truth stared her in the face.

Like that first night he visited Carla and cooked her dinner. Anna had called right when the conversation was getting good with Carla. Had Carla been paying attention, she would have noticed the troubled look on his face as he slid his thumb across the decline button while walking into the living room. He tried to make it look good by pretending to have a conversation with Ronald, but didn't she notice that he was talking so fast that he couldn't have really been talking to anybody? All she heard was him saying that she was a good one, and now she was serving it up to him every chance she got.

And then there was Anna. Anna knew good and damn well there

weren't any missed calls from him on her phone, but he'd dug his heels so deeply that she gave up on winning the argument. Then he'd so successfully deflected the conversation when she asked about Carla that she didn't even put up a fight. When will these women learn not to give up so fast? She might have busted him had she kept pushing the issue. Yet, a few soft words and a gift for Evie later, and Anna was already making dinner plans for them.

However, there was still a barrier neither woman could mount. They couldn't just let go and trust him. Not that either of them had a real reason to trust him, but it would make things so much easier if they stopped questioning him. The sex would be twenty times better. He was tired of initiating "make up sex" whenever Anna got pissed with him, and he was exhausted with Carla pretending to be Mother Teresa when they got together. If she would just learn to let go, like Anna had, maybe she would enjoy herself more. She was just too scared of being used. He'd started argument after argument with them both to convince them that they were wrong for their feelings, but he never succeeded in breaking down their walls.

He knew he couldn't blame them. He saw each woman every chance he got and tried hard to make them both feel like they were the only woman in his life. He rotated his weekend time with them, listened when they wanted to vent (which was too often for his taste), and even helped pay a bill or two when needed. Admittedly, he liked paying bills for them. It made him feel needed. He knew there were some men who got off on getting women to give them money, and although he knew he had the skills to do it, it made him feel like less than a man to take money from a woman. Besides, Anna was a single parent and Carla was a good girl. He didn't feel right taking money from either of them. He did have somewhat of a heart.

However, he wasn't ready to let either woman go. He still felt he had the best of both worlds. Carla gave him the passion and intensity he needed, while Anna gave him the challenge and sexual gratification he sought. Together, they made the perfect woman; he loved each of them for their qualities.

Yet, in all his years of being a player, there was only one woman he felt he could love fully, and it was neither Carla nor Anna. This woman held the key to his heart without even knowing it, but he'd broken her heart so badly that there was no chance of ever getting her back. He wasn't sure if Anna or Carla could take her place, but he planned to juggle them until he could find out. How long he could carry this thing on, he wasn't sure. So far, they both still thought they were the only one. He wasn't sure if they were each dealing with their trust issues or if he truly had the gift of gab. Either way, he had to make a decision soon. He couldn't play this game forever.

8

I t was Friday morning, the last day of work before the Columbus Day weekend. Carla lay in Saivon's bed, reeling from yet another night of passion as she waited for him to get out of the shower.

Saivon's love-making skills amazed her. She still couldn't make herself respond to him consistently the way she wanted, but he made up for it by pleasuring her in other ways. By the time he got around to entering her, it didn't matter that her orgasms weren't as wet as she wanted them to be. She knew the time would eventually come when she would be his both mentally and physically. Until then, she would try to enjoy the ride. Literally.

It had been four months, and she was still happy. She anticipated every moment that she spent with him with excitement. He listened with interest and compassion when she told him about her day. He understood her desire to have children one day. They made plans to travel together. She giggled when she saw his "good morning beautiful queen" texts. Was this what it was like to truly be in love? Why hadn't she felt this way with Shawn?

She turned onto her stomach and ran through her mental to-do list. She had to finish a report she'd been working on for her boss. Her meeting with with her teammate, Kellie, was scheduled for 10:30, but she decided to put that off until after her lunch date with Saivon.

A buzzing sound above her head interrupted her thoughts. She scrunched her eyes in puzzlement as she searched for the source of the noise. When she realized it was Saivon's cell phone vibrating against his headboard, she started to lie back down, but a thought struck her. *Why not answer his phone?* In the months past, she'd let it ring, not wanting to invade his privacy. But it had been four months. If he had something to hide, shouldn't it have come out by now? But then, he still wanted her to keep their relationship a secret in the office. What if it was a coworker? *Forget that! Maybe that's why I can't come,* she thought. *Stress and secrets do not do a body good.*

With that thought in mind, she grabbed the phone and hit TALK. "Hello?"

"Hello, who's this?" asked an unfamiliar woman's voice.

"This is Carla," she snapped. "Who's this?"

"This is Anna. Is Saivon there?"

"He's in the shower, Anna. May I help you?"

Silence. "Why are you answering his phone?"

"I think I can answer my man's phone," Carla snapped. She didn't know whether to be pissed or confused. Why was Anna calling Saivon at six-thirty in the morning? And why the hell was she questioning her? Shouldn't Angie have told her Saivon was seeing someone? "Why are you calling?"

More silence. "Von and I have been together since before Thanksgiving. Are you sleeping with him?"

"Yes, are you?"

"Yes," Anna replied. "I hope you're using protection."

"I don't think that's any of your business," Carla huffed. She seethed as she stared at the bathroom door, wishing she could pitch a boulder through it. She was going to kill Saivon! No wonder he wanted her to keep their relationship a secret! "How could you be seeing Saivon when he's with me every night?"

"Well, it's obviously not *every* night," Anna said with a laugh. "We're together every weekend and most evenings when he gets off work."

"Anna," Carla stated. "You're Angie's friend, right?"

"Yes, and Saivon's woman."

"I heard about how you've been trying to get with Saivon for the longest," Carla said, sitting up and swinging her feet onto the floor. The sheet fell down, exposing her bare breasts. She didn't care. "That was cute before he got into a relationship. Now I think it's time you move on."

Anna laughed, but there was no joy in her voice. "If you know Angie, then she should have told you that Von is with me and has been for a long time. Now if he had a slip up and gave you a little bit, take it for what it is and move on. You are not now, and have never been, his woman."

"Excuse me?" *No, she didn't!* Carla popped up and began pacing the room. She couldn't believe this was happening to her, but she tried her best to sound unbothered. She refused to show this woman that she was getting to her.

"Anna," she said, trying her best to sound reasonable. "I really don't want to fight with you. There are enough black women out here fighting over a man, and we don't need to add to the statistic. But why would he spend all his time with me if he was still with you? Wouldn't that make you feel neglected?"

Anna remained silent for a few seconds, but soon recovered. "Sweetie don't get it twisted. Von satisfies me every night. The only time I don't spend with him are the days when he needs time to himself. And the way I put it on him, he needs that time to recover."

That cut her. He'd told Carla the same thing when he began going out of town with his friends on the weekends. He said he needed to relax because she'd taken all of his energy. *Damn.*

The two ladies continued talking, snapping at each other as they each tried to get the upper hand. However, they soon realized that they'd both been played. Soon, they began comparing notes and filling in gaps. It turned out they knew many of the same things about Saivon, and when one didn't have him, it seemed the other did.

When Saivon finally came out of the bathroom, Carla pitched the cell phone at him and shouted, "You need to handle your shit! Why is this bitch calling you?"

She could hear Anna's voice asking who she was calling a bitch as she stalked out of the room. She was naked, but she was too pissed off to care. She'd finally found the reason she couldn't trust Saivon. Her feelings had been confirmed, and she felt more vindicated than disappointed. It was time to get out of there while she still had some dignity.

She returned to the bedroom and caught the end of a heated exchange between Saivon and Anna. He had told her he was trying to be nice, and he didn't want her calling him anymore. He then told her that he and Carla had been seeing each other for a while and asked why she was trying to mess that up. They seemed to go back and forth until he finally hung up and threw the phone across the room.

"Shit!" he yelled, pacing back and forth. He still wore the towel he'd wrapped around his waist when he came out of the shower.

Carla was unmoved by his anger. Silently, she picked up her clothes so she could get dressed and leave.

"Where are you going?" Saivon asked. Before she could reply, he snapped, "Then go ahead and leave!"

"Don't yell at me!" Carla shouted. "You're the one who has your *other* girlfriend calling me. How does she know so much about you if you supposedly never touched her?"

"She's best friends with my fuckin' co-worker!" he shouted. "What do you expect? I told you how nosy everybody is at work. Angie tells her every fuckin' thing!"

"So, I guess she knows where you go on your little weekend trips, huh?"

"She doesn't know where I go," he pleaded. "She probably knows I go somewhere, but I never told her about where I go. Maybe she found out from Ronald."

"Whatever, *Von*," Carla said with a wave of the hand. "Yeah, I know your little nickname. I don't need this shit."

She'd gotten fully dressed and had headed for the door when Saivon called after her. "I told her I loved you." She froze and turned to face him. "I told her we'd been together for a while, and I didn't want her messing things up between us. I worked too hard to get you."

She bit her lip, wondering whether or not to believe him. His words sounded good, but Anna sounded very convincing. Who was telling the truth? "I just can't see a woman holding on for this long. She said you two have been together since last Thanksgiving. Why would she stay after you for this long?"

"I don't know, Carla Baby," he shrugged, taking a seat on the bed. "I promise you I don't talk to her. She's been calling here for months trying to get with me. I guess Angie told her about us, so she figured she would call here and throw salt in the game. She told me when you gave me the phone if she couldn't have me, nobody could. And then she started laughing."

"Why didn't you tell me she's been calling you?"

"I didn't wanna cause any more trouble between us," he explained. "All we do is argue about trust and I didn't want you thinking I was messing around with her. Every time she calls here, I hang up as soon as I hear her voice. I hate her ass!"

"Don't say that," Carla said softly.

"I know *hate* is a strong word, but that's how I feel about her," he said, thrusting his face into his hands. "I don't wanna lose you. I'm in love with you. I was gonna ask you to marry me today, but after this, I wouldn't blame you if you walked out on me."

A tear stung the corner of Carla's eye. She wanted to believe him. She *needed* to believe him. But she couldn't play the fool again. "Don't lie to me, Saivon. I'm really not trying to be played with right now."

He rose from the bed and stood directly in front of Carla. He looked into her eyes and said, "Look at me, Carla. I'm in love with you. I've loved you since the first time we made love. I want to marry you. Don't let Anna's bullshit run you away."

"Those are some serious words you're telling me," she said quietly.

"I know they are."

She looked away and thought about the levity of his words. He had the perfect chance to walk away, but he didn't. Instead, he proposed. "You really wanna marry me?"

"Yes," he nearly whispered as he lowered to his knees. He kissed her stomach as he squeezed her butt. He went lower, all the time mumbling how much he loved her.

Tears streamed down her face as she once again let her heart overrule her head. Maybe Anna really *was* making things up to ruin things between them. "I love you, too."

"Girl, you will not believe what just happened this morning!" Carla exclaimed as she drove into work.

"What!" Lorraine asked with alarm in her voice. "Whose ass I gotta kick?"

Carla laughed, glad her friend always had her back. "Let's just say this day is starting off crazy already."

"What happened?"

Carla stopped at a red light. "I stayed at Saivon's place last night, and—,"

"So, what else is new?"

"Girl, shut up and listen!"

"Okay, sorry. What happened?"

"Well," Carla said as the light turned green. She continued driving and took a sip from her coffee. "We woke up this morning to get ready for work and he went to take a shower. I'm lying there waiting for him to get out, and his cell phone rings. Normally, I don't answer his phone, but something told me to pick it up today."

"'Bout time," Lorraine said. "You know I've never been a Saivon fan. I hope you found out what he's hiding."

Carla winced. She wished her friend hadn't said that. Now she didn't even want to tell her the rest of the story. Why did she have to take every opportunity to express how much she didn't like Saivon? He never did anything to her.

"So, what happened?" Lorraine pushed.

Carla sighed and continued with less animation in her voice. "I answered the phone, and it was that bitch Anna."

"What?"

"I kid you not," Carla said as she pulled into the St. John's Hospital parking garage. "She had the nerve to question who I was, and then she said she's been with Saivon for the longest."

"What did Saivon do?"

"I told him about himself when he got out the shower, and then he cursed her ass out and told her to stop calling him," Carla reported, hoping this bit of news would convince her friend that Saivon was for real.

"I don't know," Lorraine said after a moment. "This Anna chick is always popping up. You better be careful, especially since you work with her friend."

"Now, that I agree with," Carla said. She pulled into an open parking space and left the car on so she could continue speaking through the Bluetooth in the car.

"You sure you don't want to cut your losses and find somebody with a little less drama?" Lorraine asked. "You don't deserve this."

Carla shook her head as she watched a doctor walk across the garage and approach the elevator. He made her think of Bryon. Now, that was a guy with a lot of drama. She'd seen him more than a couple of times walking into the hospital with a different woman. When will men realize that their job doesn't make them the prize? They need to bring a lot more to the table than a professional job in order to be with her. She never experienced that with Saivon.

"We're getting married," she blurted, prepared for the tongue-lashing she was sure her friend would give her.

She heard Lorraine gasp, but thankfully, she didn't yell. Surprisingly, she was quite calm. "Carla, I love you like my sister. I'm not going to ask you if you're sure about this because I know you feel you are. I'm just going to ask you to please not rush into anything. Give this some time. I don't want to see you get hurt. You've been through enough already."

"I know what you're saying," Carla said. "Trust me. This time is different."

"I'm not too sure, but if you're happy, I'm happy for you."

"That's all I ask," Carla replied. "You'll see. Saivon is a keeper."

"You lying mother—" Anna screamed once Saivon walked into her house. She looked around and picked up the closest thing to her—the TV remote control—and flung at him. He ducked just in time. "I hate you!"

"Anna!" he shouted, ducking just before a glass made contact with his head. It crashed against the door. A hint of fear flashed into his eyes as he looked down at the broken shards on the floor. "Baby, listen to me!"

"I don't have to listen to shit!" she yelled as she snatched a small lamp from the table next to the sofa. She cocked her hand back to throw it, but Saivon rushed toward her and wrestled the lamp from her hand. She wildly flailed her hands to slap him, forcing him to bear hug her from behind to keep her to keep her arms down. "Let me go!"

"Not until you calm down and listen to me," he pleaded, backing them both up to the sofa. He sat down and pulled her onto his lap. Helpless, she cried as his strong arms held her like a straight jacket.

"I trusted you, Von," she cried. Her tears streamed down her cheeks. Unable to wipe them away, she tried rubbing her cheeks against her shoulders. She could feel the wet spot forming on her t-shirt. "I told you not to lie to me."

"Baby, I didn't lie to you," he said, finally loosening his grip. He scooted her around, so she faced him and took her by the wrists. Looking her into the eyes, he repeated, "I didn't lie to you."

"Then what do you call it when a woman answers your phone at six in the morning?" she asked. "What was she doing there?"

She stared at him, knowing he would lie. She expected the lie. Deep down, she *wanted* the lie. Hearing that he'd been with someone else would have been too much. But knowing that Angie and her mother were right all along, that she'd let her daughter get close to a cheater would have been worse. In a way, the lie he would tell would measure how much respect he had for her. His lie would make her feel better. It would convince her that she was right in fighting for this relationship.

She'd spent her entire day at work rehearsing in her head what she would say to Saivon when she finally saw him. He'd blown up her phone all morning, but she refused to answer it, proud of herself for sticking to her guns. She succeeded in pushing her feelings to the side so she could concentrate on the children in the center, but they rushed right back to the forefront as soon the kids took a nap.

By the time she got home, she had her entire plan mapped out. She would calmly and reasonably tell Saivon that the relationship was over, and that she would not allow him to make a fool of her. He would come up with some lie, but she wouldn't listen. It would be a simple, professional conversation. But once he came through the door with that pitiful ass look on his face and called her "Anna Baby," everything she wanted to say went out of the window and all she wanted to do was hurt him worse than he'd hurt her. Too bad she missed his head with that glass. That would have been a good start.

Saivon looked around, his hands forming a death lock on her wrists. "Where's Evie?"

"I knew your lying ass would pop up over here when you got off work, so I asked Angie to let her spend the night," Anna explained, venom dripping from her voice.

"Baby, I'm telling you I didn't lie," he pleaded again, pulling her into a hug.

She pushed him away and walked to her bedroom, slamming the door behind her. He followed her and, realizing she'd locked the door, pounded it with the side of his fist.

"Go home, Von!" she shouted.

"I'm not going nowhere!" he shouted back.

Anna stood facing the door with her arms folded. She hated him so much right now. Did he really think she was stupid? The more she thought about Carla's voice, being all smug and comfortable in his apartment, probably lying in his bed, she wanted to scream! Who did she think she was, anyway?

"Anna Baby, are you gonna let me talk to you?" Saivon asked.

"What can you possibly say that can explain that woman being in your house and claiming to be your woman?" she asked, refusing to move any closer to the door.

"The woman is crazy, Anna."

She rolled her eyes and sucked her teeth. *This* was the lie that he expected would win her back? Was he serious? "Von, you're going to have to come better than that."

"I'm serious, boo."

"Von, even if she is crazy, it doesn't explain how she ended up in your house at six in the morning, and why she thinks she's your woman." She felt ridiculous yelling at a closed door, but it was what it was. That door wasn't ready to be opened.

"Can't you just open the door so we can talk?"

"If I open this door, you will not like what comes out of it. Now, say whatcha gotta say."

She imagined him standing on the other side of the door looking pitiful. Part of her loved the fact that he was even trying to plead his case. She was sure that any other man who had been caught cheating would have left by now.

"Anna Baby, I promise you there's nothing going on with us," he started. "I-I've been working with her on a project at work. She came over last night to talk to me about some research she needed to do, and we got to talking. She was all messed up over this dude Shawn she was messing with, and you and I had just had another fight, so we started talking about our problems. I pulled out some Hennessy for myself and she asked for some. Next thing I know, we were drinking, and it was getting late, and I dozed off. I didn't even know she was still there until I woke up to take a shower."

"So, she drove all the way to your house to ask you a question that she could have asked over the phone? Really?"

"She did call me, but she came over to pick up some paperwork," he explained. "B-but when she got there, she looked like she was crying, and I felt sorry for her."

Anna's eyes shifted as she contemplated Saivon's story. Should she believe him? Lord knew she wanted to, but there were too many holes in his story. He'd never mentioned any big projects at work. And besides Angie mentioning Carla a couple of times, she'd never heard her name mentioned before. Well, she'd gotten what she'd asked for: a lie that sounded like the truth.

"Anna Baby, you still there?" Saivon asked, knocking again. "I'm sorry I put you in that situation. This is messed up in more ways than you realize."

Anna took a deep breath and let it out in ragged huffs. She tightened her fists and loosened them when she felt her nails dig into her palms. If she opened that door, there would be no turning back. Why did love have to be so complicated? Why was it so hard to end a relationship when she was still in love? She paced the room a couple of times, beating herself up for what she was about to do.

She took another look at the door, bit the inside of her cheek, and walked to the door. Placing her hand on the doorknob, she again asked herself if she was doing the right thing, and then changed her mind. "Von, I think you need to go home."

"Anna Baby," he said.

"It's like you always say," she said. "I need some time to myself to clear my head."

His response was silence. Had she run him off? Was this it?

"I respect that," he said finally. "I just want you to know that this was going to be the day I asked you to marry me. It wasn't supposed to end like this."

Anna gasped. Had she heard him correctly? Did she really start her day by catching her man with another woman and then end it with him proposing? She snatched the door open and stared at him. "You can't be serious."

"I'm very serious," he said, walking toward her. She backed up, but he continued walking forward until he had her backed against the wall. "Tell me you don't want to marry me."

She looked him in the eyes, but words refused to form. She looked away. He took her by the chin and guided it until she faced him again. "You love me?"

Tears threatened her eyes again and she nodded.

"Tell me," he demanded, stroking her cheek with the backs of his fingers.

"Yes, I love you, but—"

"No buts," he interjected. "Look, I know I messed up, but I fixed that shit. I cursed her ass out for answering my phone and trying to mess up what we have. Now I'm gonna need *you* not to mess up what we have, either. You understand me?"

Before she could respond, he locked her into an authoritative kiss that announced that all talking had ended. He picked her up and carried her to the bed, falling on top of her. She tried to pull away, but he held her in place, gently grabbing her by the throat. The little bit of fight she had left slowly dissipated as he continued kissing her and peeling off her clothes.

What just happened?

9

"**Y**ou know you owe me your life, right?" Ronald told Saivon a week later.

"Whatcha talkin' about?"

"Carla came to see me today," he reported with a smirk, leaning back in Saivon's recliner. "Congratulations on the engagement. Why you ain't tell me?"

Saivon shook his head as he walked back into the living room with two beers. He winced when he saw his friend sitting in his favorite chair. "Move, nigga."

Ronald laughed as he moved over to the sofa and took one of the beers from Saivon. "So, what's up with you and Carla?"

"I fuckin' panicked," Saivon admitted with a sigh as he settled into the chair. "She was about to walk out. That was the only thing I could think of to make her stay."

"Why would she have walked out?"

"Anna's ass called me, and Carla answered the phone."

"Aww, shit," Ronald said. He shook his head as he took a sip from his beer. "What happened?"

"They talked, compared notes," Saivon shrugged. "Carla cursed me out and wasn't tryin' to hear nothin' I had to say. I even tried some reverse psychology shit, but that shit didn't work either. I even pretended to curse Anna out for a good five minutes after she'd hung up on me. I made sure Carla heard me, but that didn't work either. So, I proposed."

Ronald doubled over in laughter. "Man, you done lost your mind! You gonna marry Carla?"

"Shit, I don't know. Maybe one day, but I ain't figured out which one I want yet."

"Well, don't you think you need to figure that out?"

"Yeah, especially since I proposed to Anna, too."

"What the fuck?" Ronald asked, his eyes wide open. He froze, anticipating his friend's answer.

"You heard right," Saivon replied, taking a deep swig from his beer. He couldn't bear to look at his friend, so he wiped his mouth with the back of his hand and stared at the TV. "Twelve years in the game, and it comes down to this shit. This shit ain't never happened to me. Not like this."

"I knew your Return of the Mack ass would get caught up one day. This is what happens when you try to play two grown ass women. When did this happen?"

"The same day. I went to Anna's house after work to explain things. She wasn't tryin' to hear me, either. The woman locked herself in her room and had me talkin' through the door like an asshole."

Ronald howled in laughter. "How did you explain Carla answering your phone?"

Saivon chuckled. "I told her Carla was depressed about her ex and fell asleep after getting drunk. I didn't even have to explain why she answered my phone. When I told her I wanted to get married, all the questions stopped."

"Damn, bruh."

"I told her I cursed Carla's ass out for answering my phone," Saivon said. He chuckled again and added, "That's when I asked Anna to marry me."

"Aww, shit," Ronald exclaimed, laughing again. "How the hell you gonna propose to two different women?"

"Fuck, I don't plan on marrying either one of 'em," Saivon said, sipping from his beer. "I got bigger problems to deal with."

"Well, I'ma tell you like this," Ronald said, leaning closer to his friend. "Carla came to me almost in tears because she really wants to marry you. She asked me if you really meant it when you proposed."

"What did you tell her?"

"I told her you wouldn't have asked anything like that if you didn't mean it and that Anna got issues," he replied. "I told her how crazy Anna was, and how she and Angie used to always hang around us trying to get us to spend time with them."

"Good lookin' out, man," Saivon said, pounding fists with Ronald. "Don't get me wrong. I wouldn't mind makin' either one of them a wife, but Lord knows I ain't ready for that yet. I only proposed to Anna because it worked on Carla. I didn't expect her to say yes so quick."

"You know all these women wanna get married. Hell, I could pick up the phone right now and propose to somebody and she'll most likely say yes. A professional with a house like mine? Shiiiiittt!" Ronald said with a chuckle. "Well, whatever you do, tread carefully, my dude. All women have a little bit of crazy in them. You don't wanna be the brotha who brings it out of them."

If only Saivon had listened to Ronald. Two months had gone by, and he was still no closer to making a decision. Instead, he continued stringing both Anna and Carla along. He had yet to present either of them with an engagement ring, yet he continued proclaiming his love for each of them.

Technically, he wasn't lying. He really did have love for them both, but not in the way they wanted. There were moments when he felt guilty about what he was doing, but those moments were overcome by the excitement he got when even his smallest lies paid off. Both women still thought he was a basically good guy, but he knew they still hadn't gotten over the phone incident.

He also knew that both women had considered leaving him at different times, but they never had the courage to go anywhere. He gave them just enough sugar to make them almost afraid to leave. They both wanted to believe Saivon loved them, so they never asked him the hard questions. They also never mentioned the other woman's name, as if the problem would cease to exist if they didn't talk about it.

He took extra precaution in ensuring that he didn't overlap his dates or mix up facts about the two women. If either of them showed frustration with him, he'd either soften his voice to sweet talk them out of their anger or he'd become enraged, flipping the script and causing them to forget about accusing him and defend themselves. That technique had worked for him since that fateful night when Tasha busted him in college. He was surprised that it still worked after all those years. He guessed even grown women didn't like shouldering the blame for the demise of a relationship.

Secretly, he wondered if neither woman wanted to leave because she was afraid that he would go to the other. Like what would happen if Carla left him and started seeing him hanging out with Anna all of a sudden? Or vice versa? He knew neither of them could handle their pride being hurt like that. And both of them really wanted to be married, so they would hang on as long as possible. Little did they know that he had even bigger problems.

Why would he propose if he was seeing more than one woman?

That was the question on Anna's mind as she lay next to Saivon Saturday morning. She turned over and watched him as he slept. Even in his slumber he looked strong and beautiful.

She had no idea why she'd stuck with Saivon for so long. It had been almost a year of ups and downs. Mostly downs. They'd had more arguments than she cared to count. He'd disappeared more than a few times. Yet, she continued to hang on. Why?

Angie had told her about all the attention Saivon bestowed upon Carla at work, but he'd vowed that there was nothing going on between them. That he was only trying to be friendly since he'd cursed her out for answering his phone. He claimed they still had to work together and that because the project they'd worked on a couple months ago went so well, they were placed on the same team again.

She tried not to worry about the incident. Things between her and Saivon had been pretty good since then. They'd spent more time together, and he'd helped her out of a couple of financial tight spots. They'd even discussed him adopting Evie once they were married.

Saivon slowly opened his eyes as if feeling Anna's gaze. "Hey, baby, good morning."

"Good morning," she replied.

"How long you been up?"

"A while. Just doing some thinking."

"About what?"

"About when we're going to have our wedding."

He was quiet for a moment, letting out a long yawn. "Soon. As soon as I get some personal things straight."

"Anything I can help with?"

"No, this is some business I have to work out with my sons' mother."

"She giving you problems?"

"Yeah, she heard I was getting married, so she's trying to do all she can to stop it. But don't worry about it. I got it under control."

He grabbed her suddenly and rolled her over until he was on top of her. "You love me?"

She smiled. "You know I do."

"Well, be patient with me. When we get married, I'm gonna make you happy for the rest of your life."

"You promise?"

"Yes," he huffed, lowering his head and kissing her.

"I tried to call you last night," Carla told Saivon Sunday morning. "You didn't go out of town, did you?"

"No, I was home," he said. "I just forgot my cell in the car, and I was too tired to go out and get it. I'm sorry."

"No problem," she said absently. "I just wanted to talk with you."

"You should have come over," he said. "I was here all night."

Yeah, I'll bet you want me just popping up on you, she thought to herself. She'd pictured him all night making love to Anna. The thought consumed her so much that she couldn't get any sleep.

Her irritation led her to dismiss all thoughts of talking to him about the wedding. She still couldn't put her finger on it, but something wasn't right. There was a reason Anna refused to leave her thoughts. No matter how much Saivon expressed his love, bought her gifts, and hung their engagement over her head, she knew he wasn't being totally honest with her.

But how could she prove it? He always seemed to have a good excuse about his behavior. If he disappeared, it was because he had to work late, or he had to help Ronald with something. She never pushed the issue because she didn't want to start an argument, but this whole situation was ridiculous. Which is why she didn't feel guilty Monday morning when she asked Angie to contact Anna so they could meet. If she was going to marry Saivon, she wanted to go in with a clear head.

Carla sat at *Friday's* nervously anticipating the meeting. The lunch-time rush was less hectic than the Friday evening crowd, but it was still loud and noisy.

Just be straight forward, Carla told herself. *This is what you have to do in order to move ahead.* She sipped from her lemonade as she awaited the inevitable. *I wish she'd hurry her ass up.*

As if on cue, Anna walked up to the table with the same air of royalty she'd shown the last time Carla had seen her when she showed up at the office and got dismissed by Saivon.

"Hello, Carla," she greeted authoritatively as she stood over her. Nothing in her stance or voice spelled friendliness. She made it clear that she was there to handle unfinished business, not make a new BFF.

Carla wondered at first how Anna knew it was her since they'd never met, but then she was sure Angie had told her friend what Carla would be wearing. Besides, there weren't any other women sitting by themselves in the restaurant. *Let's just get this over with.*

"Anna," Carla said, matching Anna's tone. She watched her sit across from her, keeping her purse in her lap as if she wouldn't be there more than a minute.

The waitress approached the table as the two women stared each other down, hatred in their eyes. The poor woman had no idea of the powder keg she was entering.

"Hello, will you be dining with us today?" she asked, setting a menu in front of Anna.

Carla's rival smiled at the waitress and ordered an iced tea.

"I'll get that right back for you," the waitress said. "Do you need a few minutes to decide on something to eat?"

"No, thanks," Anna replied, still holding her smile. "No, the iced tea will be fine. I can't stay long."

"Okay, well I'll just get this out of your way, and I'll be right back," the waitress said, picking up the menu.

Carla marveled at how friendly Anna sounded, wondering if they could be friends if the circumstances were different. Her smile seemed to light up her face, but it disappeared just as easily as it appeared once Anna turned back to face Carla.

"How can I help you?" she asked, her all-business demeanor back in effect.

Carla was a bit taken aback by Anna's abruptness, but she pushed forward anyway. "Look, I called you here to speak with you. I'm sure you know Saivon and I have been together for quite some time. I also know you have some feelings for him, but I need you to get over that. Saivon and I are getting married, and—"

"Excuse me?" Anna cut her off, her face scrunched in confusion. She saw the waitress approaching, so she waited for her to place her tea in front of her before asking, "You and Saivon are doing what?"

"We're getting married," Carla said, looking Anna straight in the eyes. "So, I need you to leave him alone."

Anna took a sip from her tea and took a deep breath. "Carla, I'm glad you called me here because we need to talk. Why do you think my name always comes up? Why do you think I call him or show up at his job?"

Carla shrugged and hardened her gaze.

"I told you before that Saivon and I have been together all year," Anna continued. "Now don't think that your little drunken sleepover is going to change all of that. He's my man and will be for a long time. I'm sorry if that hurts you, but that's the way it is."

Carla's eyes lowered into slits of hate. Desperate to channel the energy seething through her body, she stretched out her fingers as far as her skin would allow. When she could no longer take the strain, she closed hands and began tapping a rough tune with the handle of a butter knife. She knew her actions revealed her discomfort, but she didn't care. "You really need some help. Didn't Saivon tell you we were together when he cursed your ass out? I never got drunk at his place. I was there because he wanted me there, just like I always am. Stop making up stories in your head."

"What are you talking about? Saivon never cursed me out. He came to my house that night begging me to forgive him for putting us in that situation. Then he proposed. We're getting married at the beginning of the year."

Carla sat back and cursed under her breath. "That lying bastard proposed to me right after he hung up on you."

"He never hung up on me," Anna said. "I hung up on *him*. I heard you tell him to handle his shit and then you called me out of my name. I cursed *him* out and then hung up on *him*. He called me about twenty times that morning, but I didn't take his calls. So, he showed up at my house after work."

The two women looked at each other and blinked, each realizing they'd both been played.

"I don't believe this shit," Carla mumbled, holding her head.

"I do," Anna snapped. "This explains why he's been acting so crazy."

They spent the rest of the lunch hour comparing notes, each kicking themselves for not recognizing the warning signs earlier.

Carla was so pissed that she couldn't return to work. Instead, she drove up and down River Street, the main thoroughfare in Downtown Savannah, trying to clear her head. It was still early, but the clubs and restaurants were already beginning to fill. She wished she could enjoy some of the live music like she had no care in the world, but not tonight. How could she have let herself get caught up like this? Why didn't she end this thing a long time ago? Why didn't she listen to her instincts?

"Shit!" she screamed, beating up her steering wheel. "How could I be this stupid? What the fuck is wrong with me?"

It was so obvious what was going on, but she'd let love blind her. So many people had tried to warn her, but she didn't listen. She was too ashamed to tell Lorraine, who would wonder what type of pattern she was setting for herself, given her immediate prior relationship with Shawn. She'd also tell Carla she told her so, since she'd tried to convince her to leave him after the phone incident.

And then there were Angie, Stacy, and the rest of the women at the office. They didn't even like her, and they tried to warn her. Of course, she didn't listen. Everybody was wrong except Saivon, right? She'd let herself fall victim to their snickers and behind-her-back comments all for the sake of some great sex. There was no way she could go back to work and face them.

She'd talked him up to her family, bragging about how wonderful he was. She made excuses as to why they hadn't had a chance to meet him yet. The truth was he was never around to meet them. Now, she'd have to go back and tell them that he'd used her. Embarrassment couldn't begin to describe how she felt.

Rage soon took over. How could she have let him do this to her? She couldn't let him get away with this. She had to let him know how she felt.

It was nearing six in the evening when Carla pulled in front of Saivon's apartment. She'd calmed down somewhat, but her rage was still evident. She hated Saivon and wouldn't be satisfied until she let him know just how much. He always talked about crazy women. Well, she was about to *show* him crazy!

She walked straight to the front door and was surprised to see it wide open. She listened and heard voices coming from the living room. Arguing.

"Look, like I said before, things don't always work out the way we plan. It didn't work out. Just move on."

That was Saivon's voice! What was going on? She crept closer to the doorway and tried to stay out of sight.

"It's not that easy. See, you hurt me. You lied to me over and over, even after I gave you the chance to be straight with me," a woman's voice said. Damn, that's what Carla was going to say. She could hear the woman crying. She cried so hard, she couldn't make out the voice, but she figured it had to be Anna. She guessed she and Anna not only had the same taste in men, but they also thought the same. No wonder Saivon liked them both.

"You used me," the woman said. "You made a fool out of me. You care about nobody but yourself, and your ass needs to die tonight."

"Bitch, if you don't give me that motherfuckin' gun, we're *both* gonna die tonight!"

Gun? What the hell? She was about to kill him? Carla wished she could see what was going on, but she was afraid of being seen. She lowered herself to her knees and tried to peek around the doorway just in time to see Saivon lunge at Anna.

"What the fuck is wrong with you?" Saivon shouted, turning to run at her again. "You want some dick or something? Would some makeup sex make your ass feel better?"

Anna again dodged him, this time pulling the trigger. The bullet tore through his arm, scaring all three of them.

"Bitch, you shot me!" Saivon shouted, grabbing at his arm. "You got about two seconds to get outta here or else I'ma beat your motherfuckin' ass!"

Two more shots rang out. Saivon's lifeless body fell to the ground, as a woman's scream filled the air. But it wasn't Anna's voice. It was Carla's. Unable to bear the carnage she witnessed, she screamed at the top of her lungs and popped out of her hiding place.

Anna jerked around to see Carla crying in the doorway, but before she could say anything, another woman walked into the room.

"I loved you," the woman said. "I gave up everything for you. And this is the kind of bull shit you bring me into?"

"W-where did you come from?" Carla asked. Anna stood in rigid shock, the gun hanging at her side.

"I've been here the whole time," the woman said as she emerged from the bedroom.

"Who are you?" Carla asked, tears streaming uncontrollably down her cheeks.

Anna and the woman looked at Carla.

"Nikki. Who the fuck are you?" the woman snapped. She tapped her gun against her leg, seemingly ready to use it again if she heard the wrong word.

"C-carla," she choked out. "Why did you kill him?"

Nikki looked down at Saivon's body, which was still oozing blood. "We were supposed to be getting back together. He'd been begging me for months to move back to Savannah so we could be together. He told me he had changed and wanted to be a family." She turned to Anna and tightened her grip on her gun. "Then I find out he proposed to *your* ass."

Anna looked like she could hardly breathe. Finally, she whispered, "H-he also asked her to marry him."

Nikki looked back at Carla. "Ain't that some shit. Now, who the hell are you, *Carla?*"

Carla hardened her stance, her eyes shooting daggers at Anna for selling her out. How did she know the next bullet didn't have one of their names on it? She swallowed, refusing to show fear. Maybe if she seemed pissed about the situation as well, Nikki wouldn't turn the gun on her. "Looks like this piece of shit played us all."

Nikki turned and slammed the butt of her gun into the wall. "I knew I shouldn't have trusted his ass! Something told me he was full of shit."

Anna regained her composure when she heard police sirens in the distance. "I'm guessing you're Saivon's sons' mother. I don't know how you fit into all this, but we'd better come up with a plan quick. The police are coming, and we all have bullets inside of him."

"I don't!" Carla shrieked, backing toward the door.

"How would you like to have a bullet inside of *you?*" Nikki snapped, pointing her gun at Carla. "Now, the way I see it, we're all in this together. This motherfucker pulled the wool over all of our eyes, and we all had reason to kill his ass. You can try to run and tell, but you'll be dead before you hit the door."

Carla swallowed. "I didn't have anything to do with this."

The sirens got louder. Footsteps headed in their direction.

"You got about two seconds to make a decision," Nikki said.

"Police!" an officer announced, his gun leading him into the apartment. Three officers followed him. When they saw Saivon's body lying in a pool of blood, they flocked around him to check for signs of life.

The first officer looked up and saw the three women standing lifelessly in their spots. Two of them held weapons while one cried.

"Drop your weapons!" he shouted. When they complied, he placed his gun back into his holster. "Okay, which one of you wants to tell me what happened here?"

Anna and Nikki turned their heads toward Carla. She looked back and forth at them, wondering what to say. She wanted to turn them both in, but what would that solve? Should she try to cover for them?

She looked at the officer, who was now standing in front of them with his hands on his hips. She cleared her throat and said, "Thank God, you came when you did. These women..." she looked back and forth at them again, "saved my life."